To Jennie,

The Tiger

How long could he stand in this terrible jungle without moving a muscle? Cold sweat trickled down his skin, soaking his shirt and adding a shiver to the hair already standing up on the back of his neck. The closeness of the bush was made even more suffocating by the dreadful crawling insects and slithering reptiles just barely out of sight.

Jim was frozen with terror. His arms and legs were too heavy to lift. The eyes of an enormous tiger were fixed on his own. Jim knew that if he moved the wrong way the tiger would leap once and sink its teeth deep into his throat, then rip away, tearing the jugular and executing him like a professional assassin.

Except for the tip of its tail moving hypnotically, the tiger was absolutely still barely ten feet away. It had killed many times before and its primitive instinct was ready to eat. The shocking orange and black markings, so attractive behind the cage bars in the zoo, were now a vicious costume of terror.

An explosion burst out of the leaves of a mango tree at the tiger's side. The beast turned suddenly as a blue parrot flushed from the bush and away from the showdown. Jim panicked and bolted. Out of the corner of his eye he saw, as if in slow motion, the giant tiger unfold from his crouch and explode off the ground directly on a course to intercept the running man.

Jim covered his face with his hands, feeling the slash of leaves and branches as the oppressive weight of the tiger slammed him into the underbrush. He tried to scream.

THE
SAFARI
CHRONICLES

VOLUME ONE

THE SAFARI CHRONICLES

VOLUME ONE

Rick Butts

Safari Adventure Company
800-442-6214 / www.rickbutts.com

Published by:
Safari Adventure Company
800-442-6214
www.rickbutts.com

Printed in the United States of America

ISBN 0-9660981-1-0

**Publisher's Cataloging-in-Publication
(Provided by Quality Books, Inc.)**

Butts, Rick.
        The safari chronicles. Volume one / Rick Butts.,--2nd ed.
        p. cm.

        1.   Africa—Fiction. I. Title.

PS3552.U891S34 1998   813'.54
                                             QBI97-41219

From the Author

Research shows that as many as 85 percent of all the "business/self-help books" are rarely read past the second chapter. After helping thousands of people to seize their courage and take charge of their own future in live seminars around the country, I felt compelled to share what I'd learned about dealing with sudden change with a wider audience. But I didn't want the power of these magical ideas to get overlooked because they were boring to read.

Inspired by Spencer S. Johnson's brilliant and compact book, *Yes or No, The Guide to Better Decisions*, I decided upon a short easy-to-read story approach. *The Safari Adventure Company* (the original title) was the result.

Even I was unprepared for the overwhelming response to this first book, which sold out of its first printing in less than three months. People devoured it, some starting and finishing the book in a single evening. I began to get letters from people who said, "Someone gave me this copy and asked me to read it. It has changed my life!"

The Safari Chronicles is a fictional adventure to be sure. You can, of course, read this as an exciting, inspiring journey. But there is a powerful message contained in these pages. As you make your way, you ought to be aware of a couple of tricks that I, clever wizard that I am, have used to make it more fun!

First, you are best served by assuming the role of the skeptical main character, Jim. As you encounter each situation and person, try to think what you might do. By processing the story this way you will be amazed at the power of your own mind to shed light on the problems you face in your own journey.

Second, suspend your conclusions about why things are the way they are in your family, workplace, and world. We adults are the product of dozens of illusions that have ceased to serve us, but which we stubbornly cling to. Take a break from your negative assumptions; leave a crack in the dark room of your misfortune. Let a little light experiment in there.

Third, symbolism abounds! What ideas do these people, places and things represent? CLUE - anything that appears more than once is probably intentional.

Fourth, think for yourself. Think. Think. Think!

Finally, you cannot imagine how much I would love to hear from you with your observations, applications, and questions about *The Safari Chronicles*. I do not sit in a lofty tower, but concoct these dreams to share with you. Please feel free to e-mail me at rick@rickbutts.com or visit my website at www.rickbutts.com anytime.

And now settle into your favorite chair and get ready, the adventure begins!

Rick Butts
Denver, Colorado
July, 1997

Dedication

It is a fool indeed who labors under the illusion that
he does anything significant by himself.

—Rick Butts

The fifth printing of this book is dedicated to
my daughter, Rachael.

Dear Rachael,

Since the first moment you arrived you have been the most profoundly important person in the whole world to me. I've treasured each of our adventures together and prayed and fretted over your every challenge. You are clever, talented and pretty, and I am so proud of you.

The most important achievement, the highest calling and the greatest reward I can imagine is that you remember me as a good father.

Thanks for showing me
the nickel moon —
Love forever,
DAD

Table of Contents

Introduction to
Benjamin's Little Book
1895

We, the members in good stead of the Royal Safari Adventure Company, do herewith set forth our great hope that you, the reader, will avail yourself of the wisdom contained on these pages. The principles here are time-tested and strong. You need to know from the beginning that you will always be as unhappy as you are this otherwise fine day, unless you come to realize that true, fulfilling happiness does not lie on the easy path you have probably chosen so far.

If you seek fulfillment in the "things" of this reality, you are doomed to be ruled by circumstance, unforeseeable luck, and the whims of others who care not a whit for you or your lot. These will be your masters as you struggle to fill the void in your life with the stuff of materialism.

For you see, dear voyager, you will never be genuinely content until you gain the understanding that there is a higher, deeper, more profound joy awaiting the seeker. One that cannot even be glimpsed from the easy path.

There are certain joys, we call them treasures, that each of us may possess despite the winds of change that blow on us all. The Three Treasures herein will serve you well if you recall to measure and add to them every day. Neglect to care and protect them regularly, and you will go there one day to find them gone, sifted away a little at a time like a hole in the bottom of a flour sack.

We heartily encourage you to gather these treasures, for they are there for every one. Seek them and your life will be richer than any King who lies awake at night, sleepless despite his rooms filled with gold. Protect them, never let anyone trick you into trading them for the passing pleasures of this world, and they will comfort you in your golden years and put you at peace about the life beyond.

The Safari Adventure Company

On one side was a Chinese restaurant. On the other was a savings and loan. A small freestanding, red brick building housed the Safari Adventure Company, American Headquarters. The antique brass and green sign looked like something from London, circa 1800. A large glass window filled to clutter with all sorts of curious telescopes, helmets, a battered ship's wheel, and countless other interesting objects, beckoned a closer look.

Across the street, Jim squeezed the leather-padded steering wheel of his Jeep Cherokee and shouted until his lungs burned for air.

"I hate him!" he cursed, through clenched teeth. "He has got to be the most incompetent manager in America. No, wait, on the planet! That's it! What a waste of a paycheck."

Shaking his head to gain control he pushed all four power window buttons down. A blast of chilly air fresh from crossing the snow-capped Rocky Mountains swept into the Jeep.

Breathing through his nose several times, Jim tried to regain his composure. His boss had pulled another one of his famous double talks and hung him out to dry.

"Okay, let's not forget our little mission," he said out loud.

He pulled the wrinkled yellow flyer out of his pocket one more time and read the familiar words that had brought him here in the first place.

THE SAFARI ADVENTURE COMPANY

"The Greatest Adventure is the Rest of Your Life!"

Just This Once, You Owe It to Yourself to See How You Measure Up Against a Real Challenge! Choose from Many Different Lands, Climates, and Adventures.

This Is No Disneyland, This Is an Odyssey!

For More Information
Call 800-442-6214

Jim had always played it safe. Never in his life had he allowed himself to be put in a position where he might lose. Carefully playing the odds, he had constructed a false world of security. Like most of the people he knew, the momentum of mediocrity had captured him. He was only now beginning to sense the pain of realizing that sad fact.

Feeling self-conscious, Jim unfolded himself from the emerald green Jeep. He was tall, but the chatty transportation consultant, Eddie, assured him at the dealership that taller people had been very happy with the "sport utility vehicle." It was a little tight behind the wheel but he wanted the Jeep so much he bought it anyway. He just liked the way it made him feel.

He pulled up his collar up against the wind and examined himself in the side mirror. "Not bad for 41!" he said to the mirror, his blue eyes flashing their boyish smile as he finger combed back a stray black lock, flecked with silver.

Many of his friends were already bald. His forehead was getting a little larger but he still had a respectable crop if you moved it around a little. That gave him some feathers in his war bonnet around the water cooler!

It was difficult for him to quit wearing the pinstripes at first, but he started on Fridays for a while. Now he really preferred the khaki slacks and denim shirt he wore today. He straightened his brightly colored silk tie, hiked his pants up over his American paunch. The butterflies took off in his stomach as he turned to cross the street.

The heavy oak and glass door swung in easily to Jim's push, jingling the leather strapped sleigh bells used by busy shopkeepers. The place looked like a cross between a trophy den in an explorers home and an overstuffed souvenir stand at a carnival. There were posters from far away places, gifts, no doubt, from the thankful travel agencies they used for their tours.

There were dozens of trophy animal heads, fresh, and saltwater fish, staring intently from every wall. Some of them were adorned with hats, and other trinkets. Sporting a pair of giant purple sunglasses, even the ferocious tiger head had a strangely funny and harmless appearance. Instead of a fierce snarl, the tiger (God, he hated tigers!) seemed to smile. Jim smiled back.

Two voices were talking excitedly in the rear of the office. One had some kind of accent: perhaps, it was British. Within a minute of waiting, no one had come out to greet him, and Jim began to get cold feet.

The lady who had answered the telephone when he had called for information earlier had been a little evasive and would not give out many details. She insisted that Jim could not simply choose to sign up but, rather, would have to come in and apply. She told him he would have to pass a test. Not everyone could qualify.

"This had to be a big sales gimmick. The old 'take-away close'!" he thought. "They make you think you can't have it, which only makes you want it more, and at their high price! They're probably back there hammering on some poor, old soul right now." Well, he wasn't about to fall for any tricks.

Just then the trouble at work began silently poking their fingers in his chest. He tightened his jaw.

"Oh, this is stupid! I can't be running off to some crazy dude ranch," he thought, to himself. The smell of the Chinese food teased him to think of an early dinner.

Just as Jim put his hand on the coolness of the brass doorknob to leave, a sound roared down the hall and into the waiting room.

What an outrageous laugh!

This was one of those deep, rich, belly-laughs that starts with an unexpected burst and turns into a wheezing, gasping attempt to speak that is denied words by the force of whatever hilarious affliction began it all.

You can't help but laugh when you hear one of those plastic, battery-operated "giggle boxes" they sell in novelty shops, and you couldn't help but want to laugh at this raucous "haw-haw-haw" belting down the hall. Jim smiled and snorted in spite of himself.

When was the last time he had laughed like that? The happy sound, so robust and carefree, contrasted the knot of tension that seemed to live in his guts full-time. Jim sat down on the couch and decided to see this thing at least to the next step.

The coffee table in front of him looked to be made from an old ship's door. He ran his fingers over the rusty hinges and rough wood now smooth from a million coats of varnish, and picked up a travel magazine. As he thumbed through he became immersed in an article about kayaking down a river in Asia.

The water looked so blue and cold next to the bright orange kayaks and yellow outfits of the people in the pictures. Gosh, did it look exciting!

Jim had been involved in all kinds of outdoor activities as a boy. His rough tough dad had insisted the boy "learn to be a man" so off they would go, camping, canoeing, climbing. Jim loved the adventure and though his father was a stern disciplinarian the two of them always seemed to get along best when they were pitting themselves against some obstacle or deadline.

The crystal clear photographs and descriptions pulled him in to the magazine. He was right there, shooting the rapids. The roaring of the river filled his ears when, suddenly, the voices in the back room were joined by the movement of chairs. Footsteps down the hall indicated they were coming toward the front. Jim pretended to read the magazine.

"Hullo there, sir!" Jim startled at the booming voice and sat up to see a bear paw sized hand sticking out toward him. "Didn't hear you come in, I guess. Benjamin at your service, sir! Welcome to the Safari Adventure Company! And who might you be?"

Benjamin was a giant! 6-feet 5-inches tall with tree trunks for arms. He stood there with his hands on his hips. The khaki pants and vest over a plaid flannel shirt, sandy hair and full beard made him look like a backwoods trapper. The mischievous dark eyes and wide smile pulled Jim in like a target.

Jim stood right up and shook hands. He used a tighter grip than normal as he gazed upward into the bearded face. Jim was just over 6-feet tall and not used to looking up at many people. He sensed how funny it felt, like he was a kid.

"Hi, my name is Jim," he said awkwardly and stammered something about seeing the ad and calling.

"Smashin'! You'll do just great!" complimented Benjamin, which served to both encourage and make Jim suspicious of the "qualification" part.

"This here is Todd. He went on his first safari with us about two years ago. Tell 'em Todd. Is it worth the time?"

Todd was about Jim's age and wore a dark navy suit and an outrageous tie. He turned rather shyly toward Jim and grinned.

"Great tie, Todd," said Jim, smiling back.

"Thanks," replied Todd lifting up the bright silk. "The Safari Adventure Company makes these up special for members."

There was a distinct sparkle in his eyes, as he said simply, "Whatever you do, don't miss the opportunity to go. It'll change your life forever!"

With that, Todd turned back to Benjamin. They shook hands vigorously and said good-bye.

As Jim was watching Todd leave, Benjamin put his arm on Jim's shoulders and said, "Come on now, mate. I'll bet you've got a million questions. First of all, I'm Australian," and he pointed him down the hall to his office.

The office was a bit messy but comfortable. There were pictures everywhere. Jim noticed a candle burning on the back credenza and sniffed the pleasant smell of sandalwood.

"I just like the way it smells," Benjamin said. "I read the other day that one of the trends in our society is that people are treatin' themselves to small indulgences. You know, bub, flavored coffees and the like."

"Yeah," answered Jim, "I spend a small fortune on Starbuck's coffee. My grandfather would faint if you would have told him people would buy water from France in little bottles and gladly pay $3 for a cup of coffee!"

"The problem is the twenty-first century jungle, Jimmy. This crazy sped-up world we are trying to manage."

"What do you mean?"

"Technology is killing us not makin' life easier. John Naisbitt said in *Megatrends* that 'the more we become high-tech, the more we long for high-touch'."

"He was right on that one. I go down to the underground tunnel area a lot for lunch," said Jim, "The one place that is always packed was recreated from an old barn. Antiques and the like. Feels good."

Benjamin handed him a coffee cup with the Safari Adventure Company logo on the side after finding out Jim took it with cream only.

"How did you get into this business, Benjamin?" asked Jim, trying to think of something intelligent to say as the two men sat down at the desk and sipped at the steaming mugs.

"I went on a safari, of course. Everyone who works for the company started out as a customer. Once you've been on one yourself, it will be easier to see why that happens," Benjamin said pretending to straighten the papers on his messy desk.

"Have you guys been in business very long? I've never heard of you?" asked Jim.

"Oh, my word, mate, yes! The Company has been around for quite a long time. It was started in London in 1856 by a group of people who felt that the average bloke never got the chance to push themselves to their limits. Most people go through life pickin' the low hangin' fruit. You know, they get an education or some kind of trainin', then they plod right ahead into the job they trained for. Victims of circumstance. I have met very few teenagers who had any serious idear at all what they wanted to do for the rest of their lives. From time to time they get restless and go crazy, some make changes, but most live a bit of a sad, bittersweet life wonderin' if there ain't more."

If there was one phrase that described how Jim was feeling it was "isn't there more?" He even caught himself the other day sadly singing the old Peggy Lee song, "Is That All There Is?"

"I don't mean to imply that a simple hometown life is wrong. I live that life myself now," Benjamin patted his belly. "What I mean is that there is somethin' deep down inside a heart that longs to be right smack-dab in the middle of a real adventure!"

Jim nodded. This boisterous Australian was quite a captivating speaker.

"Ridin' the same elevator, lookin' at the same plant in the same hallway, year after year, sort of melts the backbone if you get my drift, Jim.

"There is a longin' for somethin' that can't be found in the ordinary go of things. Explorin' new places, seein' sights for the very first time, facin' real danger, and helpin' to be part of somethin' bigger than just a paycheck. Sometimes as a part of a team and sometimes just climbin' that last few hundred feet to the top of a mountain all alone."

Jim listened in captivated attention.

"It was true in 1856, and it is even truer today. A psychology magazine article I read last month confirmed what I've known all along. They said that 85 percent were unhappy or unfulfilled with their jobs and 50 percent would rather be married to someone else. Just look at the movies they watch and the games they play. Sex and violence, virtual reality battles, and they go out and buy a 4-wheel drive Jeep when the roughest thing they face is an occasional pothole!"

Jim's mind flashed. He thought about his fancy 4-wheel drive Jeep in the parking lot. He thought about the cable television program he had recently seen that teased about virtual reality sex.

Instantly he thought about how bored he often was with his job in the downsizing company. Boredom interrupted only by the major idiot who was his boss lying and backstabbing him.

"Do you know what I mean, Jim?"

Benjamin's words were more than statistics to Jim. He had let the game of being married to someone else creep into his mind with cautious enthusiasm more and more lately. It made him feel guilty, but he felt justified because he was sure his wife, Tracey, felt the same way. There were no money, alcohol, or drug problems, the whole relationship was more like being roommates, except they had the kids.

Jim just nodded agreement.

"I could go on for days, you know, but I can see your time is valuable. What's your story Jim?" asked Benjamin. "Exactly why are you here today?"

Jim snapped back and stammered, "Well, I got this flyer, and uh, I was wondering, you know, if this thing was for real and…"

"Lots of people see these flyers. Some call, but only a few actually come to see us."

The friendly Australian leaned forward, lowered his voice, and smiled as he looked Jim straight in the eye.

"There is another reason why you're here," said Benjamin softly. "What's really goin' on? Is somethin' troublin' you?"

The Adventure of a Lifetime

"Well, now that you ask, my marriage is roadkill and my boss is the most two-faced incompetent fool on the planet. Just a few moments ago in the parking lot I decided against a brilliant plan to kill them both and leave town, probably on a safari."

"You are genuinely clever," Benjamin laughed that bawdy laugh.

This huge bear of a man was somehow very easy to trust. Ordinarily, Jim kept things to himself but the words came tumbling out.

"All my life I have worked for this company," he began defiantly. "Saluted the powerful, dressed in the uniform of everyone's expectations, and taken my electronically transferred bacon home every week."

Benjamin grinned broadly and snorted at Jim's clever phraseology. Jim plowed ahead.

"Whenever, they needed something done I made sure my name was called," he continued. "I was a good soldier. I always believed the company would be there for me, too. Now, I'm not so sure."

"What do you mean?"

"I don't know what to do." He took a deep breath and looked down at his hands. They didn't seem to be his hands. In fact they looked older somehow, more like his father's hands.

"The geniuses at the top of our company are re-engineering now."

"Oh, you mean chopping a bunch of jobs and not telling anyone what is going on until you are marched into the slaughter room?"

"Ha! I never heard it put quite like that, but, yeah, that's pretty close," Jim said. "Rumors are flying around that the company is selling our division. The new company has a reputation of swinging the axe pretty hard and cutting the employees with tenure to bring in their people."

"I see," said Benjamin, leaning back in his chair.

"You know, downsize, rightsize, capsize, for goodness sake, you just sit and wait for someone to tell you what kind of a life you are going to have. It's awful."

Benjamin listened patiently as Jim continued to whine and flounder with his predicament. When he noticed the safari director studying him carefully he paused, annoyed.

He looked Jim straight in the eye and said, "That is certainly a difficult challenge, what do you intend to do about it?"

Jim was taken aback at the direct way Benjamin made it clear that he would have to come to his own conclusion and actions. Jim squirmed in his chair a bit and changed the subject by asking about the safari.

Benjamin explained it to him in detail. First, there would be a physical examination. The trips were indeed challenging and might include mountain climbing, rafting, hiking. Shooting safaris had been outlawed a long time ago. There would be no big game hunting. The idea of needlessly slaughtering was never a part of the original founders' plan.

Benjamin promised some out-of-this-world dining! The food would include local exotic fare. As Benjamin described delicious feasts and particularly one salted venison dish he loved, topped with a sweet date pudding, Jim realized he was salivating. He swallowed and touched the tip of his tongue to his lips slightly, and thought about the Chinese restaurant again.

The sightseeing was designed to access some of the most beautiful remote places on earth. Benjamin handed Jim a full brochure that made his mouth drop open in wonder. A big grin invaded his face and his eyes sparkled as he transported himself right there into the picture.

There would be a training seminar and preparation at their facilities before departing by plane to Africa. Once there, they would undertake the safari which would include Jeep travel to the most fascinating game preserves in the world. They would definitely encounter big game! The time in Africa would conclude with a banquet with the other safari adventurers before returning to their homes around the world. The entire program would take about 17 days.

It sounded very interesting. There was one big question left to ask. "Benjamin, how much does this whole thing cost?" Jim braced, ready to flinch at the number.

Benjamin grinned from across the desk as though this was his favorite part of the sales pitch. "It doesn't cost a dime," he said.

"What?" Jim exclaimed incredulously. Leaning forward and turning his head slightly as if he could possibly have had trouble hearing the high-volumed Benjamin, he asked, "What did you say?"

"That's right. It's absolutely free! Now, of course, you have to buy your own clothes and incidentals, but the entire trainin', food, travel, really everythin' you'll need, is provided by the proceeds of a charitable annuity that was established around 1895. It was originally financed by the founders, and has grown by contributions from graduates of the Safari Adventure Company. In fact, in special cases we even provide scholarships for some people who cannot afford to take off from their work. We pay them a salary to go on the safari, so their family can still tend the home fires."

Jim was stunned. What was the catch? There had to be some kind of a "sign-away-your-first-born" clause. But, no matter how many questions Jim asked, Benjamin made it clear there was no obligation beyond the general release of liability. Any business that wanted to stay in business would ask for that in today's lawsuit-happy society.

"Here, take the application and agreement to your lawyer, if you like." Benjamin handed him two simple sheets of paper.

"Jim, I can see that you're a little confused. So was I. You're thinkin' maybe this company, or whatever it is, may have the dough for this nonsense and can afford to be loose with it. More importantly, you are wonderin' why on earth would they offer this to the public and especially to you? Perhaps this will help.

"Jim, the person who handed you the flyer actually invited you."

Jim thought about the guy at work who had handed him the flyer. He was very pleasant and well liked. He did not seem at all like someone who would walk on the wild side with something so far out as this. Jim flashed a mental picture of his co-worker hiking the rain forest in a suit.

Benjamin stood and walked to a giant wall map of the world, turned dramatically and faced Jim with his hands clasped behind his back.

"Everyone has a hole inside them. Kind of like a void that ain't filled by anythin' money can buy, or any possession anyone can own," he said, looking Jim straight in the face. "In fact, it can only be filled by unconditionally givin' to another human bein' somethin' that he needs to receive. The people who started the Safari Adventure Company, over a hundred years ago, knew this. They, and those who have followed, want to share the experience with others that come into our path.

"About the time a person reaches their fortieth birthday they start to get real restless like," Benjamin said. "The natural rhythm of life causes them to take a long look at everythin'. They look at the past and the road they are on and ask themselves if they should continue, or make a change. What happens at that crossroads is absolutely critical!

"The brief time you take to step back and carefully make these choices could be all the difference in the rest of your life. The safari gives you the perfect time and environment to do that. If I could help you to see from this office what you will know quite clearly by the end of the safari, you would beg me to let you come."

"There was a lot to think about. An offer you can't refuse," thought Jim. Smiling wistfully, he began to feel himself getting excited about the possibility of really going.

And go he would.

Some day.

Just not now.

"Thanks a lot for your time," said Jim, rising from his chair. "I'm afraid I just cannot go at this time. Got a lot going on at the office and all. Wouldn't look too good for me to be gone when the big cheeses decide who stays and who goes, now would it?"

Jim hated himself for what he was saying. His words sounded so dumb, so foolish. But, he kept smiling anyway as he turned for the door.

"Hey look, this is an opportunity, not a commission sale. Take your time. Think it over," Benjamin said, smiling. "Call me whenever you like," he said handing Jim a beautiful business card in the shape of a treasure map. It was made of a rough parchment type paper and felt good just to hold.

"One of those small indulgences," thought Jim as he placed it in his shirt pocket.

As they walked to the door Benjamin pointed out some of the clippings and pictures on the wall. Each one had a story and Benjamin gave Jim a brief version that smacked of fun and excitement.

"We go to a lot of places all over the world. The next safari is actually scheduled to be a sort of reunion. We are goin' to Africa!" he said again with a twinkle in his eyes. "If you go you will get to meet some of the oldest members of the Safari Adventure Company. There will be people who actually knew the foundin' members!" said Benjamin proudly. "There will be a banquet at the lodge in Africa before we set out into the bush. You will hear stories there beyond anythin' virtual reality ever hinted at!"

Finally, Jim thanked Benjamin who then introduced him to a young woman at the front desk. She had been out getting her lunch when Jim came in. He recognized her voice from when he had first called.

"Yes, I talked to you on the phone!" she said excitedly. "Glad you could make it in. You *are* going to Africa, aren't you?"

She was a pretty girl in her early 20s with long brown hair and hazel eyes. Jim noticed she wore a T-shirt with the Safari Adventure Company Logo. He thought it was the coolest T-shirt he had ever seen. The jungle scene with some type of ruins in the center and animals all around was capped with the gold letters of the company at the top. Across the bottom were the words, "THE GREATEST ADVENTURE IS THE REST OF YOUR LIFE!"

"I've got some things to check on and I, uh, well, I...," his voice trailed off.

"Sure you will, Jim!" she said nodding her assurance.

"OOPS! I almost forgot!" said Benjamin, reaching into a drawer behind the counter.

"Here, this is for you. Sort of a gift for stoppin' by."

Benjamin presented Jim with a small-framed postcard-sized motivational poster. It had the word "COURAGE" across the bottom in fancy letters and one of the most striking outdoor photographs he had ever seen.

"Thanks, this is really cool!" said Jim quietly, almost to himself.

Benjamin then handed him a small pocket-sized book with a fancy burgundy leather cover. Jim turned it over and looked at the front. The title was stamped in gold foil letters and said simply *The Three Treasures*, London, England, 1895.

. "The three greatest in the world, mate. This book changed my life more than I can explain in a bit," said Benjamin.

Jim muttered about not being much of a reader, then thanked them both for everything. He carefully pulled the oak and glass door closed behind him, trying not to jangle the bells and left.

In a quiet, purposeful way, he guided his "jungle Jeep" down the long way home through the country to think about everything Benjamin had offered. The sun was setting behind him. The world was turning pink, orange and fiery red in his rear view mirror. Only darkness seemed to lay ahead. His favorite jazz station rolled out a slow mellow blues number, but Jim was an ocean away. He was trekking across a golden savannah wearing a bush jacket, boots, and a wide-brimmed canvas hat. He was parting large green leaves and peering into a clearing at some ancient ruins, searching for treasure.

A horn honked rudely as a kid in a fire engine red sports car woke him to see he was drifting into the other lane. He settled down and began to think about what lay ahead.

Benjamin was right. He hadn't realized it but he had been putting everything in his life on the table the last few months. As the soft and steady music counted out the miles, he took another look at his world.

His loveless marriage.

His painful work.

His unfulfilled life.

The hopeful safari.

The Park

"Fired!" Jim still recoiled from the sting of the idea.

Though it had happened almost two weeks ago he continuously replayed the crazy scenes that had built to the sudden outcome one more time in his mind, looking for understanding.

His incompetent boss had told him three straight lies. The first lie had burned Jim at a board meeting in front of the Vice President.

The second embarrassed Jim at a client presentation. Both times Jim had to sit there and take it or risk calling his boss a liar. Later, through mumbling apologies and platitudes about vision, strategic planning, and focus, his boss thanked him for playing along.

The final blow came when his boss pulled the rug out from under Jim in front of his own team. Here he was sitting at a conference table with his peers and the old boy announced a completely different plan than he had shared with Jim, totally disrupting the work they had been doing for six weeks.

Then he had the audacity to tell the group he had warned Jim not to do the very thing he had instructed Jim to do privately. He just hung him out to dry one too many times.

Jim looked across the perfectly mowed green grass carpet of the City Park. The breeze pushed a few dry leaves down an easy hill to a little duck pond. The dark blue coolness of the water rippled in the breeze making the three black ducks appear to be moving, though they floated still.

"It couldn't be very deep though," thought Jim, "since it was a small park and all." He sat quietly on a park bench atop the hill in his faded blue jeans and sweatshirt, watching a white-haired old man wearing red tennis shoes, Osh Kosh bib overalls and a bright yellow shirt with a Yankees' ball cap, brim turned backwards. The old timer was feeding stale bread to the highly focused black ducks.

"Fired!" he gritted angrily through clenched teeth. The anger came again.

When his boss flamed him in front of his own team, Jim sat stunned for a few seconds as everyone looked disappointedly at him. Jim realized they believed the old boy, knew Jim was not pulling his weight.

In anger, Jim turned to the boss, seated on his left, told the whole truth to which the boss stated flatly. "Jimmy, there is no need to lie and embarrass yourself further."

That did it. Without even thinking Jim whirled around and slapped the boss so hard it knocked his glasses and false teeth out on the table.

The stunned employees on Jim's team watched in horror as the old boy rescued his parts and fled the room while Jim tried to explain.

Jim sat back and thoughtlessly rubbed the dry roughness of the wood and wrought iron park bench between his thumb and forefinger. His expensive black leather scheduling planner, once the center of his universe, and the book he was trying to read lay beside him with the spine turned to the breeze so they would not fly open.

The night after visiting the Safari Adventure Company Jim had gotten a call at home tipping him off to some missing funds. The evidence pointed to his boss. Jim's boss called him in the next day to a meeting of the board of directors and, before Jim could even think, produced forged documents blaming Jim.

A federal investigation had targeted the company: they wanted a scapegoat. The powerful executives were able to turn the truth into a lie. Behind closed doors, they offered Jim a "deal."

If he took the blame quietly, he would lose his job, but they would give him full pay and benefits for one year. Cooperate and the company would not press charges. If he went to court they would fight tooth and nail with all the money and power of the corporation behind them. Jim's attorney told him it would cost a fortune, take years, and be almost impossible to win. Some deal.

It was worse than a nightmare. Jim signed the papers, cleared out his desk, shipped his personal belongings to his home and was escorted out the door by a security guard in humiliation. He could still feel the stares of his co-workers as they watched him walk the gauntlet to the lobby with his eyes on his shoes, his tallness embarrassingly obvious.

They had recruited him right out of college. He had worked for the company his entire adult life. The whole world was out of focus and everything he had ever believed in was upside down.

Compounding the crisis, his wife and children had all but kicked him out of the house. They were treating him like a criminal, and Tracey actually had the nerve to insinuate that perhaps the company report was true.

Maybe Jim really was the incompetent one, she said, coldly doubting his story. Jim's heart raced as he felt again the anguish of the bitter words. He saw the moment again. There she was, hands on her hips. Her eyes revealed confusion and the hurt she, too, was feeling. He wanted to hold her but instead had given a choked, desperate laugh, and walked away.

The lack of love in their marriage was a ready garden where the seeds of doubt and anger could now grow wildly. She was a stockbroker who earned more money than he did. It made Jim uncomfortable but they only spoke about it in teasing comments, usually with other couples at parties where he laughed along. Now the unspoken tensions of the years were full-blown nightmares he was having every night. They had been sleeping in separate rooms and he often awoke in a sweating terror. Even the dreadful and scary tiger dream he used to have as a child had returned. He was a ghost in his own house, silent and defeated.

He gazed down the hill toward the duck pond and tried to imagine his future. It was completely blank. Even his imagination seemed to be broken. It was one thing to have a mid-life crisis and buy a new wardrobe, a sports car, then start thinking about leaving your wife for the new receptionist. It was another thing altogether to go to bed quietly, safe and snug, then wake up in the middle of the wilderness!

Jim turned sideways on the bench to prop his feet up and knocked his day-planner off onto the ground. Several papers slid out onto the freshly mowed grass. The wind instantly noticed and began to scatter them across the park. He cursed wearily as he bent to retrieve his past life.

"I don't know why I even bother to carry this darn thing around," he wondered aloud. "I haven't written anything in it in two weeks, and I sure don't have any appointments to keep."

He pushed the appointment book under the edge of his leg to keep the wind from blowing it again and cracked open the small burgundy book Benjamin had given him. With a sigh he began to read the introduction.

The Three Treasures
Copyright 1895.
The Royal Safari Adventure Company
London, England.

We, the members in good stead of the Royal Safari Adventure Company, do herewith set forth our great hope that you, the reader will avail yourself of the wisdom contained on these pages. The principles here are time-tested and strong. You need to know from the beginning that you will always be as unhappy as you are this otherwise fine day, unless you come to realize that true, fulfilling, happiness does not lie on the easy path you have probably chosen so far.

If you seek fulfillment in the 'things' of this reality, you are doomed to be ruled by circumstance, unforeseeable luck, and the whims of others who care not a whit for you or your lot. These will be your masters as you struggle to fill the void in your life with the stuff of materialism.

For you see, dear voyager, you will never be genuinely content until you gain the understanding that there is a higher, deeper, more profound joy awaiting the seeker. One that cannot even be glimpsed from the easy path.

There are certain joys, we call them treasures, that each of us may possess despite the winds of change that blow on us all. The Three Treasures herein will serve you well if you recall to measure and add to them every day. Neglect to care and protect them regularly, and you will go there one day to find them gone, sifted away a little at a time like a hole in the bottom of a flour sack.

We heartily encourage you to gather these treasures, for they are there for every one. Seek them and your life will be richer than any King who lies awake at night, sleepless despite his rooms filled with gold. Protect them, never let anyone trick you into trading them for the passing pleasures of this world, and they will comfort you in your golden years and put you at peace about the life beyond.

Jim lay the book on his lap and nodded to himself. It was true that he had relied on all the outside forces in the world to make him happy. Always searching for the feeling of having "arrived," and never getting there.

Now more than ever his circumstances threatened to rule his mind and actions. He was not certain what the book meant by its treasures but he was open to the idea. Whatever he was doing now, it sure wasn't working!

A bright yellow flyer drifted loose from the back of the book and landed on the hedge nearby. It fluttered there like a small bird struggling to be free and fly away on the next gust of wind.

Jim snatched it up. It was the advertisement for the Safari Adventure Company. A thousand thoughts rushed through his head as he remembered his visit and Benjamin, the fascinating Australian.

The park trash can was a few steps away. Jim walked over to clean out the scraps of paper from the planner. Tossing the debris into the can, he hesitated over the brochure. He looked dreamily at the scenes of elephants, birds, and smiling men and women. Jim imagined wearing the cool bush hat on the head of the man on the front of the brochure. Sighing, he slowly released it and let it sink into the bottom of the rusted green barrel.

It's probably just some bored, old timers riding around in a Jeep wearing designer bush-wear. "I'll bet there's a staff photographer who'll sell you back your memories at the clubhouse later, over a few ales," he thought bitterly. Sadly, in real life, nobody ever delivers. The real thing never looks as good as the brochure.

Jim walked in slow motion back to the bench and plopped down wearily. He felt as though all the energy was drained from his life. Clearing his throat, he wondered if be might be coming down with some kind of cold.

He looked back down the hill at the duck pond. A mini-tribe had arrived. Jim watched as the mother re-tied the shoe of her flailing boy and gave him detailed instructions and warnings about the hazards of duck ponds.

The boy ran as soon as the shoe was good to go without listening to his mother's final words. She then turned and began tending and talking to her stroller passenger, a tiny little girl adorned in bows and a frilly hat. The boy soon began inching his way toward the pond while carefully watching to see if Mom was looking.

Reaching the edge, he spied a duck that had come to the edge of the pond to beg for bread. Removing his freshly tied shoes and clean white cotton socks; he stood and surveyed the situation. He looked first at the duck, then back at his mother. In one quick motion he turned and lowered himself backward down the little cement bank and into the six inches of water at the edge.

Smiling a mischievous smile, eyes wide, he stepped softly toward the trusting duck, his extended hand clinching make-believe bread. The duck floated closer. Suddenly, the duck realized there was no bread. It was a trap instead! It honked loudly, beat the water with its wings, and paddled backwards furiously.

In the flurry and noise the duck splashed and soaked the youngster who covered his face with his hands and squealed with total ecstasy at the sight and sensation!

"Stephen P. Larson!" screamed his mother, as she spun around and reached the pond instantly. Swooping the hunter up with one arm and swatting his behind in one seamless motion, she recited what must have been a "greatest hits" selection for the boy.

"How many times have I told you to stay out of that pond?" she asked, expecting no real number for an answer. She scolded and dried him with extra verses of future warnings. Eventually the young explorer was hugging her, swearing his love, and apologizing. They embraced as she kissed his damp head. Soon he was swinging on the swing set, a duck feather squeezed tightly in his hand, the trophy of the mighty deed.

Well, there it was. Stephen P. Larson knew the price he would pay for taking the risk. The call of adventure was stronger than the voice of fear. On the shore was predictable safety, but out in the pond was possibility. The boy had guts.

Jim sat and watched in silence.

The little desk poster Benjamin had given him came to mind. COURAGE, it had stated.

"If I had an ounce of that I would have beaten the crap out of my jerk boss!" he thought. His muscles tensed. Jaw tightened. "I would have taken a stand, proved myself, instead of taking the cowardly money."

"Where does the courage go?" he wondered. "When does the spirit and passion for life you had as a youth start to slowly go dim and ebb into complacent, predictable, adult scorekeeping?" His heart ached as if he could almost feel the nothingness sliding through his outstretched fingers. He needed a reason, a purpose, something! Even something to fight! Something he could hit and hurt and defeat! But all he had was a hollow wanting.

The mother was now chasing the shrieking youngster in play. Her smile and mock threats of tickling were so full of love as she maneuvered, out of breath, around the monkey bars. Her baby grinned a broad toothless grin from its box seat, tucked safely in one of her arms.

Every time people try to do something extraordinary or risky, the whole village protests. Win or lose though, they forget the moment in time, but respect your character forever for trying.

After the family played a while, they wandered around to the concession stand for ice cream and over the hill toward the parking area.

Jim sat staring as the ducks paddled deliberately across the pond to where another family had arrived.

He sat for a long time.

Then he gathered up his belongings and walked slowly to the trash can. He looked around to make sure no one else could see him, then he bent over and reached all the way into the nearly empty barrel. He pulled out the brochure and stood staring at it for a full minute.

Placing his fist behind one hip he straightened his back and stretched his spine.

He pulled a slender black cellular phone from his shirt pocket and deliberately punched in the seven digits. Placing the tiny phone to his ear he waited through the ringing until a voice boomed "Hullo?"

"Hi, this is Jim. I was wondering, is there still time to sign up for the next safari?"

Like a shot, a loud burst of joyful laughter shot out of the phone and echoed through the park.

Africa

Jim bolted upright and looked around the plane to see if others had heard him cry out. He was sweating despite the cool overhead fan of the massive 747.

He first had the tiger dream as a young boy. Then again in college. It had gone away after he got married but recently it had returned to his nightmares. Not surprising after all the emotional stress he had been through in the last month that the tiger would come to haunt him on a flight to his first African safari.

Turning toward the window, he saw the sparkling vastness of the Atlantic Ocean splashed against the pearl white sand of the Western coast of Africa. He had awakened just in time to see his first glimpse of the coast. With his nose pressed against the plastic window of the plane Jim watched as the small strip of sand immediately slid under an emerald canopy of endless jungle.

No photograph, no video, no description from a podium could begin to embrace the power and size of the land once called the Dark Continent. Jim marveled at the thought of the European explorers who had crossed it on foot to learn of its mysteries so long ago.

Without moving his head he looked sideways at the man in the seat beside him. Nothing was visible underneath the scratchy fabric of the gray airline blanket except for a shock of orange red hair.

"Great!" thought Jim, "he didn't witness whatever antics I was up to during that dumb dream."

He swallowed to clear his ears and felt his parched throat. Jim pressed the attendant light to summon a drink.

"Sir," a tender voice spoke in a low whisper.

Jim opened his eyes quickly. The remembering had turned into a snooze. "Sorry," he said.

"Your call light was on. May I get you anything?" the tall, skinny male flight attendant asked, careful not to wake his seatmate.

"I'm warning you," came a voice from under the blanket, "I refuse to pull this thing over if you have to go to the bathroom again because you drank too much!"

The flight attendant and Jim laughed at the joke, but the man under the blanket never budged.

After securing his favorite flying beverage, sparkling water and a squeeze of lime, he sat back in his seat and massaged his neck.

It would be several hours before they reached Johannesburg. There they would catch a shuttle plane to Lilongwe International Airport, in southern Malawi. The man in the seat beside him was still fast asleep but a freckled nose was now visible to go along with the orange red hair.

Jim opened his wallet and looked at the picture. It had been taken a couple of years ago at a ski vacation. It was a rare moment they shared together and Jim remembered it fondly as one of the happiest times in his life. His pretty wife was tall and athletic. She used to laugh and say she liked Jim because she was a big girl and felt awkward with men shorter than her. That always made him feel great!

His daughter, Claire, was also athletic and active. She had inherited his wife's dark hair and green eyes. Sure to get a scholarship, she excelled on all the sports teams at her high school. They were close when she was little, but she was so popular and busy now he felt like he hardly knew her anymore. She was so different now from the smiling child he saw in the photo.

His son was another matter. Roger was a smart aleck with a high IQ, but would score very low on a personality test. He loved to correct everyone. To Roger, tact was a nasty, four-letter word to be avoided. The sandy-haired, freckle-faced little nerd would probably live at home with Jim and Tracey forever. Jim thought how little time he had spent with Roger when he was a little boy, and even less now. Perhaps more "Dad" would have made a difference in the boy's life.

They sure looked good in this picture though. Kind of like an ad in a travel magazine. He had assumed the lack of communication was natural teenage growing pains. After being around the house for several days it was obvious they were taking Tracey's side in the blame game.

"People somehow seemed happier in those vacation pictures," he mused. He looked at the people in the picture and felt like they were strangers in someone else's wallet.

When he had told Tracey he was going to go on the Safari she had barely cared. She told him it would be fine with her if he would just get out of the house for a while. He had faintly hoped she would express some concern that she might miss him but there was no hint of that in her voice at all. When he had asked foolishly if she hated him, she replied, "The opposite of love is not hate, it's apathy, remember?"

He had once said the same thing to an employee at work. The young secretary had asked his opinion about a boyfriend for whom she had lost interest. He had imagined himself so clever then; he had told Tracey about his advice that evening. Now the words rang true in his own life. She just didn't care anymore. The kids had nothing to say. Their silence said much more.

The flight seemed to last forever. Jim sat and reread the letter Tracey had placed in his travel bag before he had departed. She said he was insensitive. That he had hurt her over and over with his critical words. He had made her feel stupid and unloved. How interesting, he thought. He felt as though she were the stronger in the relationship. This sure did not sound like the attractive confident stockbroker who made better grades in school and earned so much money.

She accused him of being a poor father. This really stung. He worked hard to be successful, but successful at what? Immersed in his work he had sacrificed spending time with his growing children to make the late meetings that dragged on at work or a club.

What were his peers personal lives like? Jim had always assumed that the huge sums of money they made would surely heal any temporary separation from their families. He opened his wallet. Funny, but the money wasn't the most valuable thing in there anymore. He looked at the photograph from the ski resort again. He looked at the letter. He stared out the window.

His daydream was interrupted by the voice of the captain announcing their descent into the airport. The shift in thought gave Jim a shot of excitement. Next to him, his seat mate stretched and returned to the land of the living with a huge yawn.

"Are we there yet, Daddy?" he kidded Jim.

Andy was a lot of fun to be around. He was in his late 30s with shocking red hair, a slim build, and a non-stop grin. There was no topic that was safe from the ravages of his hilarious one-liners. Jim liked the red-headed jokester. Andy had three girls and worked as a salesman for business forms and label manufacturer. He confided to Jim that the Safari Adventure Company was subsidizing his trip by continuing to pay his salary and bonus to his wife and girls, so he was able to attend.

Like Jim, Andy had been handed a piece of paper about the safari and had contacted Benjamin on a lark. It was a tough decision for him to be gone for long. He dearly loved his daughters and was already a bit homesick, though he wouldn't admit it. Andy was using the time to reflect and to try to learn more about himself. They had a lot of laughs on the flight and were beginning to build a friendship as they shared stories on the long flight over the ocean.

The plane descended into a surprisingly modern airport. The group stayed together and stretched their legs while their bags were loaded on to the shuttle plane. Smiles were all around. Though a little weary from the long flight, they were troopers and kept a positive attitude. Benjamin gently guided them with affirmations of what was next at each juncture.

The flight to Lilongwe, capital of Malawi, was short and easy. As they walked down the ramp, their bags were loaded into two Land Rovers by uniformed attendants. There were five passengers in each Jeep. Andy and Jim were in one and Benjamin joined the crew in the other.

"My name is Kamuto!" announced the driver. He was in his mid-20s, smiling and looking dapper in his gold and black chauffeur hat and Colorado Rockies T-shirt. He lived in Lilongwe and owned his own Land Rover. The idea of owning your own business was new and exciting for him. The recently deposed "President for Life, His Excellency Dr. Bandu," had restricted such activity and Kamuto was very proud of his entrepreneurship.

The Jeeps rolled along through the edge of town. In the distance the capitol city could be seen. Its 1960s style office buildings, cathedrals, and starch white frame houses stood out as a stark contrast to the African landscape and the mountains in the distance. They traveled along increasingly rougher roads as they headed southwest through the southern end of the great Rift Valley.

The countryside was alive with gold and brown grass fields that stretched forever, alternating with patches of forests, scrub, and under brush. They had only been on the road for about half an hour when they spotted a large herd of Nyala, a large graceful antelope. There were hundreds of the bright orange, black, and tan creatures that sprang majestically. With each leap their horns (should he call them antlers?), long and straight like a pair of unicorn swords, pointed to the sky with regal and primitive beauty.

Kamuto passed a water bottle around the cab and everyone realized how very thirsty they were.

"Hey! Do not drink too much!" He shouted to the group with a big toothy smile. "I'm not stopping every five minutes for you kids to go to the bathroom!" he kidded good-naturedly with his African/British accent.

"See?" Andy laughed heartily and smiled across the Jeep at Jim. "I told you to watch that!" Then he began telling jokes to the driver who was a fresh and willing victim for Andy's favorites. They were laughing at regular intervals only stopping for Andy to repeat the joke so the driver could tell it later and laughing at it all over again.

Jim smiled, too. Everyone was looking out the windows. Their thoughts arriving and departing at 200 miles per hour. A monkey scooted up a tree as the Jeep approached.

After an hour or so they stopped at a roadside fruit stand. There they stocked up on delicious mangoes, bananas, and pineapples—the mangoes costing less than one African cent! As they pressed on they saw more and more wildlife including endless birds of beautiful color and plumage and many different breeds of antelope.

"Look there!" called Kamuto, pointing out his window, "there in the distance."

Everyone stopped chatting and looked to see three elephants standing near a clump of acacia trees. Oohs and aahs were everywhere as suddenly more than a dozen giraffe walked out of the trees just a few hundred meters from the elephants. "Now you have officially been welcomed to Africa!" announced Kamuto loudly. "You have seen elephants!"

Finally, they arrived. The Kudya Discovery Lodge was just outside the Liwonde National Park. It was an enormous and picturesque place. The huge porch wrapped all the way around the building and was lined with wicker chairs and little teakwood coffee tables. You could practically hear the tall tales that must have been spun here by courageous pioneers and eccentric adventurers.

Everyone thanked Kamuto and bid him farewell as they gathered their bags, happy to be anywhere, at last. Jim and Andy bounded up the steps and crossed the porch eagerly.

As soon as they entered the wide, open doors, they stopped to take in the panorama of excited activity. There must have been fifty people talking and gesturing excitedly as they shared stories and introductions.

Smiles and laughter were everywhere. Those that were not in groups were moving up and down the staircases that bordered the high-ceilinged great room on either side. It was an absolute museum.

There were trophy heads of every conceivable creature lining the walls. African shields, spears, ornate feathered masks, pipes and tribal vesture pervaded every surface. More treasures even hung majestically from the huge bare rafters overhead. Everywhere space allowed, a photograph of some past adventure was squeezed in. The pictures were amazing. As Jim looked more closely he could see that the obviously modern, color, friendlier poses replaced the stern, masculine ones that reached as far back as the previous century. Across the room to the left was an enormous front desk staffed by clerks attired in bright red uniforms checking in the last arrivals.

"Mister Jim, you are very welcome here," beamed the English accented African clerk after Jim introduced himself. "You will be staying in room number 27."

"Who is my roommate?" asked Jim.

"A Mister Weinberg it seems, sir."

Jim tried to imagine what a Weinberg might look like. While Andy was getting his room assignment Jim turned and caught a glimpse of himself in the gigantic mirror right next to the bell stand. He studied himself carefully at first, pulling his bush jacket up a bit and tugging up his fatigue pants.

"Hey," he thought adjusting his Safari Adventure Company ball cap, "I don't look too bad!"

When he caught himself smiling at the man in the mirror he laughed out loud. It was such a happy laugh and felt so good he just closed his eyes and let it go. He then realized what he was doing and sobered up quickly, looking around to see if anyone was staring. They weren't. They were all too caught up in their personal excitement to single out one of their own as peculiar! He turned back to the desk clerk, still grinning.

"OK, 27. Here's your key—Mister Jim. You may want to shower up first. Dinner will be from 6PM until 10PM." smiled the cheerful clerk.

"Four hours for dinner?" questioned Jim. "Why so long?"

Benjamin stepped up to his side and answered. "Jim, there's a lot of dinner, and much to tell. You will be hearin' stories from some of the old timers of the Club," he explained. He leaned closer to Jim and whispered, "You will hear things tonight that that could only happen in Africa!"

Benjamin had walked up as Jim turned to pick up his bags. He was in the company of an athletic young woman in her mid 30s who looked like she was not a happy camper. They had been introduced to Karin on the plane. She had gotten into at least two arguments with the hostess over the food and the in-flight movie. Karin was an interesting study with her light brown hair in a ponytail and her designer shorts, shirt, and hat with matching luggage. She looked like she had been a cheerleader in college and was very attractive. Her beauty, however, was overshadowed by a foul disposition.

"What a terrible flight!" was her opening remark. "The ride in those awful Jeeps was worse, though. I think our driver hit every rock, pothole, and monkey skull between the airport and the gate!"

"What kind of spider is that in your hair?" asked Andy, reaching toward the top of her head.

"Aaaaggghhh!" screamed Karin slapping her head like Curly of the Three Stooges. "Get 'em off me, get 'em off me!"

Andy burst out in laughter as the others smiled to realize he was only joking. Karin socked him in the shoulder and gave him the most disapproving look she could.

They all shook hands and agreed to meet downstairs later before dinner and headed off to their rooms. Jim made his way to the second floor room admiring the sights and atmosphere of the place all the way.

Placing his bags on the empty bed he checked out the luggage of his roommate; black leather and very expensive. A worn copy of *The Three Treasures* lay on the nightstand. Jim picked it up carefully, turning the cover he read the inscription.

> *"To my dearest companion Weinberg. May your life run to overflowing with these priceless treasures and may you have the boundless joy of giving them away to someone else as I have done with you."*
> signed, Colonel Hampton, Featherwood—1966

The sound of the turning key caught Jim by surprise. He quickly replaced the book on the nightstand and turned to face the opening door. In walked Weinberg. He was in his late fifties, but exceptionally fit and healthy. In fact, he practically glowed. He had a medium build and charcoal gray hair.

All other impressions took second place to his dark piercing eyes. Friendly, but intense, they looked as if they could see right through you and into your soul. Not in a spooky way, but see someone for who they really are. Jim liked him before a word was spoken.

A warm gentle voice with a slight English accent brought power and dignity to the simple words, "Jim, it's so very wonderful to meet you!"

"Thanks, great to be here!" Trying not to be awkwardly formal Jim asked, "What shall I call you, sir?"

"Weinberg, of course," he answered giving Jim a wink and a silly thumbs-up.

The two took an immediate liking to one another. Weinberg told Jim that he had been in camp for four days preparing for the safari. He explained that he was a long time member of the club and would be on one of the teams as a fellow hiker.

"The safari uses a smashing concept," Weinberg said, excitedly. "We pair up green peas. Oh, forgive me, that is what we call our first time hikers! Anyway, we partner up newcomers and veterans. This gives us all a chance to meet new people and share ideas. I will be happy to be your personal guide!"

"Great!" said Jim. "Works for me."

"There will be a banquet tonight. You are in for a real treat! Tomorrow morning you will rest up from the jet lag and all. In the afternoon there will be a bit of an orientation; then off we go!" Weinberg continued.

Jim was glad to hear about the rest time. He was already feeling a little fatigued from the flight but the adrenaline was pumping from the fascinating atmosphere and excitement of it all.

After they had talked for quite some time, Weinberg suggested they go to the overlook for the show.

"Show? What show?" asked Jim.

"Oh yes, I have forgotten this is your first time here. Every evening just near sunset an entire herd of hippopotamus came out to graze on the lawns of the lodge. It is a sight you simply must not miss!"

Heroes and Legends

Weinberg was right, it was an amazing experience to watch these monstrous creatures graze gently like cattle. Jim had only seen hippos in the movies, covered up to their eyeballs in water. The mother and baby won the adoration of the group who sat in hushed appreciation at the south end of the porch.

As the sunset turned from scarlet to bronze little gaslights were set aflame all around the area by the staff. They left the porch and were instantly hailed by a group of adventurers seated just inside the dining room.

"Weinberg!" the group called out in unison, then burst into laughter at their chorus.

Weinberg responded loudly, "Hello, you bush babies!" giving his signature wink and thumbs-up. "I want you to meet my new friend and first time safari man, Jim," Weinberg announced proudly as if Jim was one of his closest and dearest friends. The whole group stood politely and greeted Jim as if he were the Prince of Wales.

There was a Dutchman in a tuxedo. An American from Detroit who shook Jim's hand firmly and told him how fortunate he was to be rooming with Weinberg. The others agreed with vigorous nods and "indeeds." A young Japanese man was introduced as a "green pea" escorted by his uncle but Jim did not catch his unusual name.

The obvious leader and elder statesman of the group was Edward Pennybrook. He must have been nearly eighty but his energy and gusto masked the fact. They all deferred to Pennybrook whenever opinions were given, never crossing words with him, but nodding thoughtfully instead. However, there was little seriousness tonight. They were old friends catching up on jokes and Pennybrook was in the thick of it. Lowering his voice, he drew them in, and began:

"A man was driving through the countryside in rural America when he noticed a farmer holding a pig up to a cornstalk as the pig ate from it. The man thought this was very unusual so he pulled his vehicle to the side and rolled down the glass.

'Hello there my dear fellow!' he called out. 'Wouldn't it save some time to throw the corn on the ground?'

"To this the farmer looked up and frowned at the man. 'You city fellows are so dumb!' he sighed, 'What's time to a pig!' "

The group erupted, howling with laughter. Pennybrook shrieked harder than anyone at his own joke and then fell into a coughing and gasping fit that set the whole group off again as they whacked him on the back.

"Pennybrook, tell the monkey and the piano again!" shouted the Dutchman after Pennybrook had stopped coughing.

"Lad, I just told it a moment ago, didn't I?" questioned Pennybrook with false modesty.

"Yes, yes, you did, but Weinberg and Sir Jim were not here," he reminded.

"Tell it again, tell it again!" egged on the others enthusiastically.

Pennybrook was in heaven. He leaned back and made a very serious face.

"Once I walked into a pub in Southampton and sat at the bar and ordered an ale," he began quite factually. "Over in the corner there was a man cheerfully playing the piano in a peppy style, although there were only a couple of patrons in the whole of the place.

"Interestingly enough, there was a monkey sitting on top the piano wearing a little suit and derby that matched that of the piano man. The bartender brought the ale, but as I reached for it the monkey jumped down from the piano, ran over and leaped up on the bar, drank my beer right down, wiped his mouth on his sleeve and slammed the mug back on the bar.

"It happened so frightfully fast that no one else saw it. Before I could say a bloody word the monkey was sitting back on the piano as if nothin' happened. It's not like me to to raise a row, so I just ordered another ale. Before I could get to it, though, the bloody monkey came and did the very same thing!"

Jim was already laughing as the Englishman made a pantomime of the dramatic way the monkey wiped his mouth and slammed the mug to the bar. The group was in ecstasy and laughed all the harder for having heard the joke already.

"Still, not being from around these parts, I lets it go and orders one more beer. The little booger beat me to it again and actually stared at me after he finished my ale. He seemed to be daring me to do anythin'.

"So, I strolls over to the piano player—he's playin' away—and taps him on the shoulder. He looks up and smiles and says, 'Hullo, mate, what can I do for you?'

"I says to him, 'Excuse me bub, but do you know your monkey drank my beer?

"He smiled back at me without stopping his tune and says, Don't think I do, but if you hum a few bars, I'll bet I can fake it!' "

Another explosion of laughter rocked the table. Someone spilled his drink in his lap and ran off to the rest room to regroup.

The Japanese men shouted "do you know your monkey drank my beer?" over and over as they slapped each other on the back and howled sending new waves of laughter over the whole table again.

Jim laughed along with the ancient jokes. He had heard them long ago as a child, but it didn't seem to matter tonight. Pennybrook continued to preside over the group until they were joined by a tall elegant blonde German lady named Nina. Though she too wore safari clothes, she exuded an obvious European elegance.

She was in her later 50s and instantly stole the spotlight with her charm and stories of the European Safari Company she had helped operate in West Berlin for the last 20 years. Nina was so well read and educated that the entire level of sophistication went up 100 percent in the group when she joined them. Jim was very impressed by the class shown by the group and their versatility in conversation.

Soon, however, she caught them all off guard with a sharply funny political joke that sent the group into a controlled giggle and then they were off again with the fun. This continued through a sumptuous dinner of exotic foods that came in multiple courses of small but delicious portions. Jim enjoyed himself immensely but only after proper identification of the ingredients!

As coffee was being served Jim noticed some people had gathered on the riser at the center of the hall. Three men and the German lady, Nina, were seated in large wicker rattan chairs facing the group. The man at the microphone must have been the oldest man in the room. His massive swirl of cotton white hair made him look like Einstein with a beard. He was dressed in an off white linen suit with a bright purple African flower in the lapel. Looking out over the happily chatting people with some satisfaction, he smiled and cleared his throat intentionally, calling the group to order.

"Ladies and gentlemen," he began in grand ballroom style, his deep rich bass voice made you want to immediately sit up straight in your chair.

"I now call to order this gathering of the Royal Safari Adventure Company Society. Welcome, and most gracious regards to our honored guests and members. We are positively thrilled to host your attendance at this most *formal* occasion!" At the word "formal" his eyebrows and the corners of his mouth went straight up. He swept his upturned hand in a presentation gesture toward the only person clad in a tuxedo, the elegant Dutchman. The Dutchman stood and bowed in majestic fashion. The audience laughed warmly at their dear friend who enjoyed surprising everyone whenever possible. At his bow the laughter turned into applause.

"We especially want to recognize our first time adventurers. Will all the people making their first ever safari please stand." Jim slowly stood self-consciously and was joined by about twenty others. He looked for his American teammates and saw Andy across the room, seated next to Benjamin. Andy smiled broadly and made one of the funniest faces possible. Jim beamed back as the veteran members cheered wildly, encouraging the newcomers. It was an exhilarating feeling to be here in the company of such incredible people!

Jim and the others sat down quickly and the speaker began again.

"My name is Arthur Kipper and I have been a member of the Club for 65 years. Two months ago I celebrated my 91st birthday and I had considered foregoing this trip because of my age. Others phoned and convinced me not to let my youth detain me! Weinberg, in fact, said that if I stayed at home the Americans would call me a 'weenie.' Would someone please tell me what that means?"

The audience showed their love with applause and cheers.

"Now that I am here among my dearest friends, I am thrilled to touch the wood on the banister to the old staircase, to see the photographs I have loved since my youth, to smell the air and flowers again. Here the years melt away. My friends, if you are granted the grace of a long life such as I have had, you will one day understand what it feels like to have the heart of a youth in the body of a seasoned citizen!

"It is long ago, yet it seems only recently that I sat in this hall, like many of you here for the first time tonight; a green pea. I was brand new, excited, nervous and quite in awe of the men and women who surrounded me here. That night there were people in this room who had seen things we read about only in books today. With their own eyes they saw new worlds. They forged history with their own hands. Men and women who had explored this country long before there was technology to make them safe.

"There sat people who had accompanied Amundson and Perry to the poles of the globe. At my table were companions who had traveled alongside Albert Schweitzer and Stanley Livingstone, and still others who had fought in the American Civil War. People who had lived lives so far beyond the average…my friends, their names will never be in the history books because they were behind the scenes, doing it! They were genuine heroes!

"There I sat, a wet-nosed lad, wondering why these extraordinary people would take the time to take us on safari. There would be no money, no property, no fame, but, there would indeed be treasure! They came to give back to this noble effort. They gave their time, their hearts, their talents, to this timeless chain. They were passing the torch of the one true light that has come into the world and we are here to pass that same light on to these men and women who have come here just like you and I!"

The crowd erupted in spontaneous applause. Standing as one they thrust their fists into the air and shouted their approval. Stepping back from the microphone, the elder statesman joined them by shoving his arms aloft and smiling broadly. After a moment, he returned to the podium and continued, "But it is not like me to be so wordy." The crowd chuckled. "I want to introduce to you now, some people who will share their wisdom and perhaps, if we are fortunate, a tale or two about the safari ahead."

First, he invited to the podium an oriental twig of a man named Songh Singh. He began with a joke about his name. Jim was fascinated as he shared the view of an Eastern man about the wonder and beauty of Africa.

"The ancient proverb says that 'as iron sharpens iron, so one friend sharpens another'," he said. "I am referring to my deep appreciation for the honor of sharing my life with some of the members of this company. It is said that we are becoming the average of our five closest associates in life. If that is true, and I believe it is, you could do no better than the people here tonight.

"The power of nature and physical exertion, blended with these friendships, has been the garden in which I have found spiritual enlightenment. This understanding has been a light on my path, an internal compass that shows me which way to go when there are no maps.

"You see," he continued thoughtfully, "my life was once very tedious and without meaning. My marriage was bitter and filled with constant disagreement and misunderstanding. I believed all my problems were caused by the external influences in my life. The government, the work, my wife, my parents, my customers were all my antagonists. I used to say 'all my problems talk back!' Then my dear friend taught me to understand The Three Treasures."

With this he turned and bowed to the sandy haired American man on the platform. The man wore a Cleveland Indians baseball jacket and jeans. He looked to be in his late 50s, and was ruddy and tanned. His face looked like leather, but his eyes were clear and bright. He nodded back gracefully.

"*The Three Treasures* were only a beginning. They started me on a mighty journey, no, an adventure, that powers my life even to this day. After the safari, I set goals for my life for the very first time. You who are new must ask yourself what you want your life to look like in five years. Have you ever done this?

"You see, my father was a fisherman. His father was a fisherman. His father before him was a fisherman. It was always understood that Songh Singh would be a fisherman too. There was just one problem. I hated fish! My friend heard me complaining about my dilemma and said to me, 'Song you are not a duck! You are not one of God's machines.' He showed me that the duck must fly north for the summer and south for the winter. Without exception, his fate, his destiny, is set in stone. You, however, can go in any direction you choose. In fact the only reason your life does not change is if you choose to keep it the same.

"I realized that the influences that I thought were controlling my life were only doing so because of my permission! I seized this idea and made new choices. You see, I had always been fascinated by electronics. I worked hard and went to school at night to learn what I loved. I read books, I apprenticed for free at repair businesses and eventually I got a new job in the business I loved. I then set new goals to own a business and now I do own a rather modest copier company."

Weinberg elbowed Jim, "Modest? Songh is worth millions!" he said. His company is not in the United States, but he has large customers in all of the Pacific rim nations!"

"In the end we must realize that our lives are brief, very brief. To simply survive is an insufficient challenge for modern times. The real challenge of a human being is to make their life truly valuable. This, interestingly enough, is begun from the inside, where all real value is fostered, and brought into a functional reality only as we give it away. So, to you who would get the most from this time I say, listen well to your companions. Especially listen to the thoughts between the words. Listen for the heart and the spirit and gather these treasures for life!"

Jim applauded enthusiastically. He thought about the truth of becoming like your five closest associates.

Weinberg patted him on the shoulder and smiled.

Jim reached across the table and wrapped his fingers around the ice water glass. It was cool and wet to the touch. Sweating, as Andy would say. As he drank deeply the cold water seemed to invigorate his entire system. He felt totally alive.

Nina from Germany addressed the group next. She talked of her first exposure to the Safari Adventure Company as a young girl. Her father was an earlier member and ran the Company location in Berlin for many years. She talked about the business side of the Company and how the investments were doing extremely well. The Company was very wealthy and contributions continued to pour in. There were plans to expand and offer many new opportunities to share the ideas that had touched so many lives to people all over the world who would not or could not take the time for the safari.

Jim learned how the club was structured and how far reaching the influence of the group was. He was impressed at the very strict discipline and high degree of accountability that they applied to all they did. It was amplified by the fact that the overall impression was one of fun and adventure, not rules and regulations.

"Discipline," said Nina, "is not a prison wall, but instead it is a framework to assure freedom."

Finally, the last man was introduced. Kipper simply called him Armstrong, and invited the muscular American to the microphone. The blond-haired, blue-eyed man in the baseball jacket walked confidently to the podium.

"What words could I add to these?" he wondered aloud, thoughtfully. "To share this time with the brilliant Nina, my beloved Songh, and the legendary Kipper is an honor and privilege.

"Tomorrow you will begin a journey unlike any you have ever taken. The mentoring process where you will each be assigned an experienced companion has been very effective and most enjoyable. I think you can sense that from the words shared by everyone tonight. We encourage you to have fun and be creative.

"However, I must warn you. Hear me well. You may have been lulled into a sense of playground amusement park mentality. This is not such a place. The African jungle, despite our roads and preparations, is still a very dangerous place. The Jeeps each have a radio and a high-powered shotgun and each of you will be given a pistol. The particular area we are in is inhabited by lions, leopards, elephants, and several other extremely dangerous and unpredictable animals. You will be given some basic training to identify many of the plants and insects that can cause harm so remember your training and stick close to your guides for assistance and advice.

"There have been rumors of poachers in the area of the Nyika National Park. We have requested the local authorities to be vigilant in their efforts to rid the place of this menace. If encountered, these men would be extremely dangerous. They protect their turf like drug lords and are usually tied in to the local community by their relatives. They are tough to catch. Do not try to interfere or be a hero. If you encounter these types: steer clear and report in later. They will be avoiding you, to be sure."

After making several additional routine announcements, Armstrong relaxed a bit.

"I have to tell you that there has not been anything near a serious accident in over ten years. We go to great lengths to keep the safari safe.

"I also have to tell you that many years ago I was on the safari that had the accident. One of the newcomers was constantly trying to take off into the bush. He wanted to fling his machete and hack into all these impossible places. His companion wore himself to a frazzle trying to control this person but to no avail. They realized they had lost track of the young man one day after lunch. The entire group searched for two days before we finally found his remains. He had been attacked by a lion and devoured. The clothing and pack were all that was left to identify the young man. It is indeed a very dangerous place to be foolish. But a wonderful place to the wise. As the great prophet once said, 'he who has ears, let him listen!' "

After the speakers had concluded, the men and women of the Safari Adventure Company broke into ever changing groups. They busily renewed old friendships and made new ones. The "green peas" were backslapped, hand shaken, and encouraged to call themselves members now. The veterans made them feel as though they had been a part of the group for years.

As it grew late Jim realized how tired he was. He bid everyone good evening and climbed the stairs to the room. Hot water burst from the faucet in a solid hard stream.

"Oh man," Jim moaned with gratitude, "hot water is one of the few things that feel this good and isn't sinful!" He toweled dry and slipped beneath the soft cotton sheets.

He was in Africa.

He was in this incredible lodge.

Before he turned out the light he pulled his copy of *The Three Treasures* out of his bag, turned to the opening page. He never felt the little book plop down on his sleeping face less than three minutes later.

The Lake
of Stars

Jim opened one eye and realized where he was. Weinberg was already up and gone. Jim peered at his watch and realized it was almost noon! Splashing some water on his face he dressed quickly and headed downstairs.

Walking through the large doors of the dining hall, Jim was absorbed by a noisy crowd of people filing through the buffet of delicious looking food. Jim was ravenous and went straight to work deciding and choosing the first plate.

He fell in line with the others and stretched his arms high to wake his muscles that were still sore from his sleep-a-thon. He heard his own name and looked down to see a smiling face looking back up.

"This is some place, yes?"

It was the young Japanese man he had met the night before. "I'm sorry, in all the noise last night, I did not catch your name," said Jim.

"My nickname is a bit unusual. I am B.B. Chang, Jim."

"B. B.?"

"Yes, my uncle is a big fan of American blues music. His favorite is B.B. King."

"Gosh, that's funny!" said Jim as they both laughed. B.B. had a great sense of humor.

"I can't believe I'm really here," said Jim. "I just woke up. How about you?"

"I, too, slept like a stone. As tall as you are, you must sleep like the log!" he said to the much taller Jim. "It is not like me to be the most lazy one. I have never been in a plane so long! I think you call it 'jet legs'?"

"Yes, that's it." said Jim smiling at the funny mispronunciation.

After filling their plates with various fruits and rolls, Jim and B.B. grabbed the nearest table.

"I am to be in Group 12. How about you?" B.B. asked him.

"Hey, I'll be with you! I'm in Group 12 too!"

They both began to talk excitedly at the same time. Laughing, Jim invited B.B. to go first. He was a quality manager in an automobile manufacturer in Japan. He had twin girls at home, teenagers.

"My wife and I are having a difficult time with them," he said smiling. "Teenagers today are so different, so materialistic, they want to have everything the parent has. They do not understand that it took their parents years to gradually accumulate possessions and knowledge as well as privilege."

Jim nodded in agreement and told about the Nike's Claire just had to have that cost over $160.

B.B. countered with the painful price of American blue jeans. "Let us form an international trade agreement."

"Great, I will send you blue jeans and you send me tennis shoes!"

"The villain is television and its relentless advertising," said B.B. Chang flatly. "My father say, 'television is awful and should be removed from the house, except if there is a big game on!' "

They laughed and understood how much they had in common. The loud clanging of a bell interrupted their discussion. Silence fell across the large dining room. Turning toward the noise, they saw their host, Arthur Kipper.

"At this time we must begin to ready ourselves for our journey. The vehicles will depart in one hour to Lake Malawi. Please be on time. You will have one hour to finish your meal and pack. You must report to the buses located just outside the main lodge. Now, before we undertake our journey, let us give thanks and ask for guidance with a prayer. Benjamin would you do the honors?"

Benjamin removed his bush hat and cleared his throat.

"Prayer!" Jim thought. "They only did that at football games and banquet invocations." He looked around slyly to see what others were doing. Most just sort of bowed their head so he did the same thing, still looking around with one eye.

"Dear God, we stand here before you today certain of two things." began Benjamin solemnly. " One, that we're not you, the one true and livin' God, and two, that we're not all we ought to be yet. Let us be filled with the power that only comes from you to learn, grow, change, and become the kind of people you can use.

"Help us to build new and lasting friendships to strengthen us in the years that lay ahead. Protect the people here throughout the safari and throughout their journeys. Bring everyone home safely. Thank you for your love, kindness, and grace. Amen."

Jim was not a religious person. He hadn't been to church in years and suspected most churchgoers were either right-wing hypocrites or kooks. Was this some kind of psycho-babble cult? His suspicion meter went up immediately. He would watch carefully. No one would take advantage of him!

Quickly finishing their breakfast, Jim and B.B. parted long enough to go back to get their knapsacks and gear for the trip. Within moments Jim was back in front of the main lodge, searching for his bus. Weinberg was already on board when he arrived.

"Hullo, sleepyhead," he said, good-naturedly. "Are you rested?"

"Yes sir, I am. I feel great," said Jim taking the seat he had been saving for him. They chatted easily. Andy soon joined them.

"Are you ready for the trip, Andy?" asked Jim, happy to see his buddy.

"I am fed and watered and ready to go!" Andy called back as he plopped down on the seat next to Weinberg. "Hey, B.B., how are those *jet legs?*"

B.B. waved and joined them. "Legs are good!" he said, patting his knees and smiling.

Andy had been the one to explain jet *lag* to B.B. who had found the pun to be hilarious. Andy had such a good funny bone he could even explain jokes in other cultures!

Benjamin and the others soon arrived. The bus pulled out and headed past the teal waters of Lake Malombe and down the valley to the southern end of the third largest lake in Africa, Lake Malawi.

The driver popped an audio cassette of some local singing group that was absolutely magical. The melodic rhythm had everyone tapping their feet to the bouncing bass line and trying to sing along with the happy chorus. Though they did not understand a word of the language the energy of the group was definitely on key!

"Dr. Livingstone, the Scottish missionary, did a lot of work in Lake Malawi. He was the first European to set eyes on this lake back in 1859. It is the third largest lake in Africa. Livingstone loved it so much, he called it the Lake of Stars. It is a beautiful blue spot on the planet with white sandy beaches and all kinds of wildlife, especially birds," said Weinberg. He was a bit of a history buff and seemed to know all kinds of amazing facts about lots of places. They all listened as he continued.

"Under the surface is another universe. There are actually more species of fish here than any other fresh water lake in the world. There are private lakeside cottages at the site where we are headed. They are all made from native materials and quite charming. During our three days there we will be able to choose from many activities designed to view and experience this wonderful place so few have ever seen."

Benjamin added, "Weinberg is right. There are catamaran cruises to the islands and fishin' villages. There is a scuba diving school or you can snorkel. Either way is excellent for viewin' all the beautiful flippers."

"That's for me!" said Andy, puffing his cheeks, pretending to hold his breath and swim to the laughter of the happy group.

Time melted into distance and soon the bus had arrived in paradise. Jim put his things in his cabin and took a brief walk down by the lake. It was warm and inviting. He pulled his new old favorite hat off and gazed at the joyous activity. There were already others there swimming, windsurfing and sailing small one man sailboats near the lodge. Dinner would be served soon on the verandah overlooking the lake up at the main area. He returned to the cabin to wash up and change clothes before joining the others.

The evening became the night as the group continued their good-natured fun and revelry. Jim and Andy settled on the wide verandah and talked as the staff lit large torches around the entire area. The firelight lent its ancient comfort and magic to the cool evening air. Jim breathed deeply of the forest and lake.

A large wooden backgammon game was on the table nearby and Andy pulled it over and set up the pieces. Jim leaned over the board and smiled, relearning an old game he used to play for hours with Tracey when they were young and broke.

It was so relaxing and peaceful here, Jim decided to let himself forget about the problems that seemed so confusing at home. "Just for now," he thought, "I am going to enjoy not worrying. Tomorrow there would be enough to do."

"Red or black?" asked Andy.

"Red. I am always red!" Jim smiled as he pulled the rattan chair up to the board.

The First Treasure

The next morning Jim was up early. The sun had just started to embrace the camp with its warmth. He sat on the rough sawn plank steps outside the cabin and opened *The Three Treasures*.

THE TREASURE OF THE MIND

Your mind or thinking process, is the starting point of any significant success you will ever know. If it is muddled, cloudy, and fraught with the baggage of lies and negativity from your past you are doomed to live inside a blueprint of a circle of unhappiness; always expecting the worst and being unsurprised at its predictable arrival. Like an ox at the threshing wheel you will continue to walk the same sad path over and over without knowing any better.

You need to understand right now it is not entirely your fault that you are here at this particular point on the map of life. You have undoubtedly been helped to arrive at your current state by misguided and unwitting accomplices. It is, however, imperative that you realize clearly that you need not remain.

Each fall, as the days begin to grow short, the bird will answer the call of the Creator to take wing and head south. When the winter begins to subside he will turn north again and grace the northern latitudes with his announcement of springtime. When the fall comes he will do it all over again. He has no choice. He is a physical machine of God's nature. You are not a bird!

You can totally change your life forever starting today, and the only reason it will stay the same is if YOU CHOOSE NOT TO CHANGE!

One cannot choose to depart for a destination if he knows not of the place. Here is the land of the mind. To become a better thinker you must be challenged by something significant to think about. The reading of books is the best investment you will ever make to life changing. Within the pages of a book one may know firsthand the struggle of another person's lifetime and the answers they have found. Real answers paid for with a thousand sleepless nights and incredible investments of time and effort boiled down to a few pages. The sights, sounds, and emotions of battles, adventures, and faraway lands for the tiny sum of a few hours in a chair by a lamp. If you do not read, you are little better off than the savage who cannot read!

Conversation is the next tool of the wealthy mind. Not the coarse, vulgar, and idle chatter of the dimwitted.

Instead, we urge you to seek opportunity to meet and learn from great philosophers. They are everywhere. People of experience and substance. Attend plays, lectures, and be frequent at the clubs and establishments such as will attract someone who can change your life. By this we mean a mentor. The people who have grown to such great heights in their insides will be generous to give it away. Not to fools who spill the precious knowledge on the way out the door, but to eager seekers who demonstrate their sincere desire to grow.

One hour spent in the company of such a one will be more beneficial than any year in university! Be patient in this search and know that the fit between two people will happen, seemingly quite by accident, and will be better seen in hindsight as to the ease with which this great event took place.

WARNING! The greatest hazard to possessing this treasure is the temptation to fill your treasure chest with worthless things. The world is changing rapidly around us and the voluminous wagons full of information and advertisements are everywhere assaulting our clarity. We must learn to separate the trash from the treasure and not waste valuable mental resource and time on the things that not only do not help, but actually pull us down the opposite path."

"And be not conformed to this world; but be ye transformed by the renewing of your mind, that you may prove what is that good, and acceptable, and perfect will of God."

—Romans 12:2.

If there were one area he had ignored in his quest for social status, this treasure hit the nail right on the head. He had not read a book in a long time. In fact, if he were honest with himself, most of the information he got was probably trash. Commercials, advertisements, and useless conversations about meaningless topics at the office.

There were precious few quality conversations with his children. Tracey and he used to talk a lot about dreams and feelings but now their communication was limited to mostly managing their commitments and money. As he closed *The Three Treasures* he decided to find and read a good book. Maybe Benjamin could recommend one.

Jim breathed in the aroma of the trees that surrounded the camp. Passing a cabin, he smiled at a lady who joined him along the path to the little open-air amphitheater where Benjamin was going to give a special workshop. They chatted easily along the dirt road lined with its split rail fence.

He could not honestly remember feeling this good since he was a boy going to the lake with his dad. His health and energy were fantastic. Andy was already there and waved Jim over to a seat next to him on the back row. Andy liked to sit in the back row and whisper little remarks and puns that kept Jim and whoever else was around laughing, including the instructors. Everyone liked Andy.

They had become fast friends and shared some powerful insights with one another around the large wooden tables in the lodge by the fireplace. Their backgrounds were completely different. Jim was Mr. Corporate America with the formal education. Andy was an ex-rock and roll musician. He bragged that he attended the College of Musical Knowledge and the School of Hard Knocks. Like two *Titanic* passengers who had been traveling in different classes in the ship, one in luxury, one in steerage, their background mattered little. They were now both hitting the icy water together and had everything in common!

Benjamin stood and greeted the group. Standing at the front of the amphitheater with the bronze sunlight streaking across the gentle waves of the lake behind him he looked as if he were an ancient philosopher plucked from another time. He had added to his familiar khaki and plaid outfit an Australian bush hat. Jim captured the scene in his mind and wished he had a camera.

"Good morning campers!" Benjamin began, as usual, with his gusto and smile. He did not usually teach classes but instead focused on counseling and administrative matters. It was good to see him here this morning and the group was eager to spend the time with him.

"I promised all of you that we would be sharin' some information that you could use not only here but all the rest of your days. Of all the wonderful things I have learned since associatin' with the Safari Adventure Company one of the most incredible has been learnin' to set and achieve goals.

"Now most people roll their eyes when I talk about goal settin' cause they've heard it all their lives. Not many actually write their goals down and what they call their goals are no more that a wish list. I like to say that sayin 'I wish' means it's just a dream without energy behind it. Somethin' you want but are not willin' to do what it takes to make it happen.

"I didn't harness the power of goal settin' until I learned a simple way to actually do it. This here is what I will share with you this morning.

"Now when I say 'get it' I want you to say 'got it' and I will say 'good!' Let's try that now."

"Get it?" he said leaning forward to bait their response.

"Got it!" shouted the group enthusiastically.

"Good!" said Benjamin with a big smile.

"Step one is to take a blank sheet of paper and write a master dream list. On this list try to get at least fifty items. Things you would like to do, places to visit, possessions, experiences you want to have, skills you want to learn, and achievements that are important to you. Where do you want to be, what do you want to accomplish in the next ten years?

The important thing here is to get the juices flowin' and go for quantity. Just a word or two will be enough. You don't have to write a paragraph about everythin'. Just get it out there on paper. I will give you about fifteen minutes to make a first list.

"Get it?"

"Got it!" they shouted, smiles everywhere.

"Good! Let's go."

Jim popped out a few things he wanted to buy. Golf clubs and small things. Then he stopped. He had never sat down and thought about where he wanted to be in ten years. His whole life had been dictated by the "track" at the company. He sat in embarrassed silence as the scratching sound of pencil and paper captured dreams all around him.

Andy poked him and pointed to the most recent item he had written.

"What is the Air Aces?" asked Jim.

"They take you up in a fighter plane and you get to actually fly the plane, with an instructor, of course, and have dogfights and all kinds of cool stuff!" he said excitedly. "I have always wanted to do that."

Jim nodded and smiled. Andy did not lack imagination.

Benjamin surveyed the group and asked no one in particular, "What would you like your life to look like on a daily basis? What activities, what kind of work, what kind of life do you want? If you don't plan it for yourself, you will always be a part of someone else's plan."

Jim added some vacation spots and other small items but he was agitated by the idea that he could not come up with a major life goal or dream. He was unemployed and uprooted from his field. What would he do when the Safari was over? Benjamin's voice interrupted. Had fifteen minutes gone by so quickly?

"The next step is to place a number next to each goal. A number 1, 3, 5, or 10, will indicate if this is a goal you intend to reach in one year, three and so on. Let's do that now. If you find you have a lot of 1s and 3s and no 5s and 10s it may be that you are shortsighted and not willin' to face the big picture. If, on the other hand you have all 5s and 10s you may be puttin' everythin' off to some far away future and not takin' action."

Jim looked down at his 1s and 3s and frowned.

Benjamin pressed on. "Then I want you to take the top four goals for each time frame, your top 1s, top 3s and so on and transfer them to a separate page. Let's start with our top one-year goals. The best way to select them is to ask, If I could only achieve one of these, which would I like for it to be? Then one more until you have your four.

"Then I want you to write a few sentences about each goal. Describe it in detail. Also, you should add the reasons why you want to achieve this goal. The reasons why are the power behind the action you will need to take to get where you want to go. Frankly, if you lack reasons why you do not have a goal at all and you will never do the necessary work to make it a reality."

"Get it?"

"Got it!"

"Good!"

The group went back to work with excitement now. Jim observed the faces. Some were smiling, some had furrowed brows and serious looks. Jim wrote the instructions down but did not do the exercise. He looked over at Andy's list. He was working on an income goal for his sales for the rest of the year. His reasons why were numerous and powerful. To provide things for his wife and daughters, and the self-esteem that it would bring, would be strong motivators when the days seemed tough and he felt like quitting.

Benjamin's voice called him back to the exercise.

"The next step is to write a game plan for each goal. What actions do you intend to take, what books can you read, what classes can you take, who can you talk to or take out to lunch and interview, what kind of person must you become in order to earn the right to accomplish this dream? Plan it and lay it out in little steps. Remember, you eat an elephant one bite at a time!"

Andy made a sound like the trumpet of an elephant and everyone laughed loudly.

"Then, you must track your progress on a regular basis. Set up a chart to review your numbers, how many pages read, how many miles run, whatever you are accomplishin'. The devil's in the little numbers. Here is why.

"Imagine we're all boardin' a beautiful sailin' ship that is sittin' in New York Harbor bound for London. Three days out, the ship is forty feet off course. Now that is a rather small adjustment isn't it? But, do you know, that if the captain never watches these little numbers and therefore never makes that slight adjustment, by the time he gets across the sea he can be a thousand miles away from where he ever intended to go?

"I see so many people who have a goal, and even think up a plan to get there, but the little things in life push them off course. Then one day they are 30, the next mornin' they are 40, or 50 and their lives end up a thousand miles away from where they thought they were goin'."

Benjamin's voice seemed to break as he looked away wistfully across the lake behind him and then back to the eyes of the group.

"Don't let that happen to you! Set your goals. Believe in yourself and your right to live your dreams. Keep workin on your plan to make it happen.

"Finally, I want to share a magic secret that will give you incredible power in this quest. Every day, do somethin', no matter how small, toward accomplishin' your major goal. The one goal, that if you accomplish it, will have the most significant impact on all the others. Read a few pages in that book. Pick up the phone and order a brochure on that class you have been meanin' to take. Schedule a lunch with someone who is already successful at what you want to become. You take these simple steps and you will truly see, the greatest adventure is the rest of your life!"

"Get it?"

"Got it!"

"Good!"

---

* Get the seminar handout FREE on rickbutts.com and use this easy method for discovering your goals!

Truth in the Library

Most of the others spent the next day exploring the fascinating lake area. Jim had asked to meet Benjamin after dinner in the library. Benjamin reserved one of the little study cubicles in the back so he could talk with Jim without disturbing any others.

They walked past long rows of old books to the dark oak study, and closed the door on the burgundy-carpeted room quietly. It was softly lit and sparsely decorated with antique furniture. A little writing desk with a green shaded banker's lamp and a round lion's-footed table in the center. Rows of books filled shelves all around.

"You said you wanted to see me, Jim. What's on your mind?" Benjamin said openly.

"First, I just want to thank you for inviting me here. I've already had a tremendous time." said Jim.

He listened to himself excitedly describe his experience at the camp in that strange way you can be talking and yet hearing yourself. He knew he sounded a bit like a kid, but who better should he express his joy about the camp than to Benjamin?

The two men talked for half an hour about the Safari Adventure Company and the upcoming trip. Then there was a moment of silence, the awkward kind where both people realize they were not listening but thinking of something else and didn't know quite what to say next, or who should say it.

"Benjamin," began Jim in a calmer tone, "I had a real problem with the goal setting workshop yesterday morning."

"What was your concern, Jim? Did you disagree with the concepts?" said Benjamin.

"No, the concepts were very sound to me. I used to do a lot of strategic planning on my job. Your ideas were great," said Jim.

"Then, what was troublin' you?" Benjamin asked again.

Jim sensed the same concern and clarity Benjamin had shown the day he interviewed with him the first time he entered the Safari American Headquarters. He knew it was safe, even wise, to be open with his friend.

"The problem was not with the workshop. The problem was with me! I couldn't set any real goals. I couldn't see any direction for my life. I have lost my job. I have been discredited falsely. My kids are ignoring me and my wife has practically disowned me!" Jim looked up at Benjamin. The pain in his eyes was easy to see.

"I got hammered and it was no fault of my own." Jim complained bitterly. It was hard to describe how confusing it was to be so happy with the safari and so miserable inside.

"Simple does not always mean easy, Jim. Sometimes things go wrong. You can either let your life story be told by what happened *to you* or what *you chose to do* next!" Benjamin started. "I'm sure it's been hard but you need to remember that this jam you're in is only temporary."

"I guess I will get another job somewhere. I know I made a mistake, but why can't I set new goals? I just went blank when we did the master list. What's going to happen to me after this fantasy trip is over?" Jim interjected, his anger poorly disguised. He was beginning to honestly feel the feelings that were being put off by all the activity and hope of the trip.

Benjamin continued with a caring smile, "Jim, it is going to be very difficult for you to see the big picture of your future until some of the clutter is cleared from today. Anyone undergoin' such a significant emotional event, like you are, would have an awful lot on their plate to deal with. Do you really want my advice on this or do you just want to talk it out?"

"I already have a great 'talk it out' partner in Andy. We have had some great conversations. I would like some advice. Have you got any how-tos?" Jim asked hopefully with a little smile.

"Okay, here goes," said Benjamin, drawing a deep breath. "You need to know that *time* is needed for you to get clarity. You have undergone a real crisis in your life and it is not over. There are two obstacles compoundin' your situation.

"The first one is external. It has to do with your family, your job and your social situation. You have always taken these for granted. They were just a part of the landscape of your life. You didn't have to do much to maintain them. Now they are cavin' in on you because you don't have the crutch of your job to brace them up.

"Your desire to put your world back together again is extremely stressful because it's practically impossible. You cannot go back into the past, though it's natural to long for a time when things were predictable, even if they had their own pain and unfulfillment."

"Yeah, I did pretty much hate my job anyway," Jim agreed.

"When I first met you, you told me the company was probably going to lay off a bunch of people. Was that fear better than this?" Benjamin asked.

"I see what you mean."

"We often tend to forget the truth about the past when the present begins to challenge us. You must accept the fact that your external world must be reconstructed and it is goin' to take time."

"Okay, what's the other thing?"

"The second obstacle is the greater. That obstacle is *you*," Benjamin stated bluntly and nodded in Jim's direction.

"What do you mean, me?" Jim shot back defensively.

"You are in danger of withdrawin' into a pity-pot. Feelin' sorry for yourself and blamin' your situation on others," said the big Australian leaning back in his chair.

"Hey! I didn't start the problem at work. I didn't alienate my wife and kids. If anyone has a right to feel sorry for himself it's me!" Jim protested.

"I will be the first to agree that you are in an unfortunate situation. You must understand clearly that the road to happiness is not goin' to be found by tryin' to fix other people. Blamin' is a waste of time. If you want to get back in the game you must take responsibility for your own life. You will be the one who stands up and takes the steps to rebuild your world. You must accept that things are the way they are and now you must fearlessly operate in that reality."

Jim started to speak, but Benjamin lifted a finger for Jim to wait for him to finish.

"We feel happiest to the degree in which we feel in control of our own lives. You must now get it straight that you are the primary captain of your own destiny. The courage, strength, and faith to go from this crossroads in your life to a place of peace and contentment will be found in new understandin', mate," Benjamin declared.

"Understanding what?"

"Albert Einstein said, 'The significant problems we face today cannot be solved at the same level of understanding in which they were created,' " quoted Benjamin. "You must grow beyond knowledge and data and seek wisdom, my friend."

"But, I don't even know which way to go," Jim said again, throwing up his hands sadly. "Where do I begin start?"

"I know this sounds too simple, but for now, but there are two handles you must grab hold of that will give you stability. Patience and time, Jim. Give it a little time."

Jim slumped back in his chair.

"Number one, if you will focus on taking responsibility for yourself and the role you played in your situation you can then begin to go about correcting much of your so-called misfortune."

"Me?" What did I do?" moaned Jim, now sitting up to defend himself.

"Come on, we all play the biggest part in our reality. Haven't you taken actions that put your marriage and parenting in their current status?"

"Well, yes."

"What did you do to prepare for your career future? Did you study, take classes, read books, network, or just wait for the inevitable "them" to do with you as they chose?"

"I guess I could have done more."

"And couldn't you have…"

"Okay, okay, I get the picture."

"Then take responsibility for the part you played, analyze what you must do now and begin to seize control of your controllable circumstances and trust another power for the rest."

"Another power?"

"Another power."

"A good place to start is the book I gave you, *The Three Treasures,*" Benjamin said. "Have you read the book?"

"Yes, I have been challenged to start to read again and learn a little, you know, improve my mind," said Jim. "All that religious stuff seems unnecessary, though."

"Do the verses bother you, Jim?" asked Benjamin.

"Not anymore," Jim responded, realizing Benjamin often answered his questions with a question, but not really sure how to turn it around without saying so.

"They are actually very thought provoking. But, I'm not a very religious person Benjamin, are you?"

"What do you mean by a religious person?"

"I guess I mean someone who thinks they are better than everyone else because they are such a "Holy Roller" and goes around criticizing everyone else for having fun." Jim realized as soon as he said it what a cliche this was.

"Is that what you see when you look at me?" Benjamin asked in a non-threatening way.

"Gosh, no, Benjamin! I mean, hey, you know, you're all right. You don't go around telling everyone how to live. Everyone admires you. Where do you stand on religion?"

"Listen mate, I have a great regard for the spiritual, not much of what passes for religion."

"How about the Bible then? I will agree it's got some good stuff in it, but do you really believe its true?" he said.

"Absolutely," nodded Benjamin. "That is exactly what I believe."

Benjamin walked to a book on the middle shelf and opened it. He began to show Jim how the Bible was created by dozens of writers who wrote independently of each other over hundreds of years without any contradiction. He showed him how the monks had preserved the writings for centuries. The pains they took to preserve the accuracy of these sacred handwritten manuscripts was incredible.

He explained how they would count every vowel and consonant forward and backward. They totaled the words and letters and found the middle word and middle letter of each chapter and each book. Erroneous copies were destroyed. Meticulously they labored in love, their lives devoted, and sometimes sacrificed, to their legacy.

Jim was impressed with this big, rough, safari trainer. Not only was he very knowledgeable, but you could tell he had a strong faith in what he believed. Jim realized he personally believed in very little of what you might call, absolute truth. Everything in his world was relative.

At least Benjamin believed *something*. Although Jim didn't understand Benjamin's beliefs: he was fascinated by ancient knowledge and sacred writings.

"I tried to read the Bible once," said Jim remembering his days in a college philosophy class. "It was boring and hard to read, with all the 'thees' and 'thous' and weird names. I just gave up."

Benjamin looked Jim squarely in the eye and said, "Mate, you will never realize what you have been missin' until you read the Bible for yourself as an adult. The history and all this are mere pips on the radar screen compared to the power you will find for your life."

"Uh huh." Jim agreed patronizingly.

"That's what *The Three Treasures* is all about at the heart of the matter. Look, Jim, no matter who is in the White House, where you live, or what is goin' on in your life, you can have these Three Treasures in abundance to bring you joy and value. They don't depend on external circumstances. Nothin' in life worth havin' is external.

"You don't start anythin' at the finish line. You start at the beginnin'. You're goin' through an awfully tough time, Jim. You must have faith and believe there is an answer," Benjamin encouraged.

"But I have no faith, I have no belief," said Jim.

Benjamin became serious in his tone, still smiling he said, "Here, then, start by believin' in belief and havin' faith that there is something that will supply that faith. If you reach for these ideas you will find what you are lookin' for, guaranteed!"

"That makes no sense to me," said Jim. "All my life has been based on facts and observable information. That may have worked for ignorant peasants but modern people see reality."

Benjamin paused, smiled, and took a deep breath while Jim relaxed. The king-sized Australian was as gentle as a lamb.

"Then tell me, Jim, where has your reality method got you now?" he replied softly.

Jim was busted.

He let out a low pitiful chuckle and said, "Standing in a pile of doo doo."

Benjamin slapped him on the back and laughed that loud raucous bellowing laugh Jim had heard the first day at the headquarters.

Jim grinned like he'd won a prize.

"Faith," began Benjamin when the laughter had quieted, "begins with a strong suspicion."

The words pierced Jim's thoughts like sunlight instantly blazing through a cloud. In that special moment something broke loose in Jim's subconscious. He was suddenly aware that the foundation he had relied upon his entire life might be unreliable.

His face revealed his emotion.

Benjamin sat silent, motionless.

At the same time he doubted the former, he became keenly aware of a restless suspicion that Benjamin might be right. That there may be a larger power and truth that undergirded and ordered all of reality, unseen to his "modern mind." The effect was at once unsettling and exciting.

"This suspicion, like a clue," Benjamin continued as he studied Jim's puzzled face, "must be investigated. Then you must make a decision, take action, and there you will find the answer."

He had only scratched the surface of what Benjamin had shared but his strength to believe a new truth for the first time depended not on him but on the truth itself. It was borne on the spirit of its own power, set aloft by the certainty of Benjamin's knowing.

"Thanks, Benjamin," Jim said sincerely. "I have practically no idea what you are talking about but I am willing to investigate. I am still in a bit of a fix, though. What do I do in the meantime?"

Benjamin smiled and said, "It's just a *mean* time!"

"Oh. Ha, ha," Jim smiled weakly.

After bidding Benjamin good-night in the library, Jim walked alone down by the amphitheater. The burning torches across the lake made a tiny golden ballet of light in the dark rippling water.

Jim lay back on the benches and looked up at the infinite number of stars in the cloudless African sky. The power of the created universe swept over him and begged for his attention. There he opened his heart to the possibility of a happiness that did not depend on circumstances, money, or any of the other things he had hoped would tell him he was good enough. It made absolute sense.

Yes, it was possible.

It felt that right.

Everyone was asleep when Jim slipped quietly into the cabin and tiptoed past Andy to his own bunk. He lay down in his clothes to rest for just a moment and sleep came quickly.

He dreamed again of the tiger. It was so vivid. The shocking orange and black colors rolled silently across the muscular frame of the ferocious killer. Yet this time Jim was not afraid. He heard the parrot's wings and saw the whole thing happen both in slow motion and in a fraction of a second.

This time there was someone else right beside him. They were moving toward the tiger. He did not recognize the older man who protected him but he felt safe because of his presence. The jungle turned into his living room at home in that strange way dreams do. The rest was lost.

Don't Call Home

Standing in line the next morning to use the pay phone, Jim began to get nervous. This would not be an easy call. Tomorrow they would head into the bush and there would not be another opportunity until the end of the safari.

The man in front of him said his good-byes and hung up the phone. He nodded to Jim as he passed. The phone felt warm from all the handholding as Jim gave his credit card information to the operator. His heart rate went up double as the distant yet familiar ring of his home phone came to his ear. His daughter Claire said hello.

"Hi, Claire," called out Jim hopefully.

"Daddy, is that you?" she asked.

"Yes, it's me," he laughed and started to tell her about the upcoming safari.

"I'll get Mom," she said and dropped the phone to the table without waiting to hear his reply. Her rejection stung like the harsh sound of the phone falling. All he could do was shake his head silently and try not to get mad.

After a few moments, he heard the sound of voices arguing down the hall. Footsteps came closer and gave way to the sound of the phone being retrieved (from the floor?). Tracey's voice asked, "What is it?"

"Hi, honey," Jim tried to begin positively.

"Don't you 'hi honey' me, Jim. What do you want?"

"We are breaking camp here in the morning and will be in the bush for the next ten days. I will not be able to call until then and I thought you would want to know."

Tracey cut him off, "Is there anything else? I am very busy," said Tracey flatly.

"Tracey, you knew I was going to do this from the start. When I signed up you said you didn't care what I did and would be glad I was out of the house for a…"

"Listen and listen good, Jim," Tracey interrupted, "I have had it with you and this whole thing. Our friends think you are nuts and the people from the plant keep calling to ask questions. I am tired of all this. But, most of all I am tired of you."

"I've changed since coming here. It has really done me so much good, you'll see," Jim pleaded as he looked around to see if anyone could hear him shame himself.

"I have had time to think, too, since you have been there. I think we would be better off apart and the kids do, too," she continued coldly.

"Aww, Tracey, come on, the kids? Calm down and let me explain what is going on," he said.

"Did you read the letter? That explains what's going on. I am not seeing anyone else. (Jim's mind went reeling at that; he hadn't imagined his wife would even think of being unfaithful.) I just feel like we'd be better off apart," she declared.

"Come on, let's just talk. The time I am here will help you think more clearly," Jim tried.

"I am thinking clearly—more clearly than ever before. Please don't try to come home now either. We would just fight. Let me take this time to think, Jim. I just need some time to think." At the last few words her voice broke and Jim could hear her trying to hide a crying sound with her hand over her mouth.

"Oh, Tracey," Jim started to speak but the phone went dead.

Jim realized she had hung up on him. Hurt, angry, and frustrated he slammed the pay phone down on the hook and growled angrily, teeth clenched. Turning around he realized there was a lady in a light blue jogging suit waiting to use the phone. They smiled politely at one another and looked away quickly. She stepped past him and up to the phone.

Jim heard her say, "Hi, honey!" to the person on the other end. "Oh I miss you, too! You are just going to love this place! We have got to do this together next time!"

Her happy words stung Jim's heart. He could feel the energy draining and the bitter anger burning in his neck. He clenched his fists as he walked away to nowhere.

He did not notice Andy until he put his hand on Jim's shoulder. Jim whirled around, revealing his distress.

"Hey buddy!" Andy shook his friend. "What did you do, eat a lizard?" he said looking at Jim's painful face.

"Oh, hi Andy, how are you?" Jim asked automatically.

"Better than you, it looks," said Andy, changing gears instantly. He could see this was no time for comedy. "What's going on?"

"Aww, I just tried to talk to Tracey and she really tore into me."

Andy put his arm around Jim and shook him roughly as he laughed. "Come on, let's get a cup of coffee and you can tell me all about it." The two men turned and headed back up across the camp to the lodge.

The Wilderness

"Hold on a minute!" shouted a familiar voice. Andy ran up to the group out of breath.

"I just wanted to say good luck and have a tremendous time. I will be taking another route with Benjamin and his team. We will meet up again at the canoes on the river," Andy said excitedly as the two men shook hands warmly.

"Good luck to you, my friend. I hope you have the adventure of a lifetime," said Jim. "Oh, Weinberg, don't let Jim play with any African Tigers."

"There are no tigers in Africa," said Weinberg matter-of-factly.

"I know that," said Jim, embarrassed, "he's just kidding."

Andy turned and trotted back to his group calling, "Hey! Benjamin! I got dibs on the shotgun seat!"

Jim turned to continue listening to the instructions of the guide. Gabriel was a native African in his mid 30s, tall and muscular with a serious face. He wore tan shorts and a sleeveless bush shirt that amplified his powerful build. Jim worried that the young guide may lack experience.

"Do not be fooled by the warm humid weather here at the bottom of this valley," warned Gabriel. "We are going to climb steadily the next two days through the highlands of the Nyika National Forest. The elevation here at the lake is 470 meters. We are going to go to all the way to 2300 meters. The weather can get very cool and unpredictable. Take the proper clothing. We will be entering a vast forest. Nyika means 'wilderness,' you will soon know why."

Jim patted his bag, remembering his thicker bush coat, and made a mental inventory of all he had thought to bring.

"This is Stephen," announced Gabriel as he gestured toward the even younger man standing just a little behind him. Stephen was very dark complected and wore a moonbeam smile and a golden earring. His red bandanna and Houston Rockets T-shirt made him look as if he had walked right off the streets of any American city.

"Hello, good to meet you all," he said with a sterling British accent as he stepped up confidently toward the group.

"So, you are a fan of the Rockets?" Jim asked Stephen.

"A what of the who?" Stephen replied with a quizzical expression.

"Never mind," said Jim.

Jim looked around at the others. There was the smiling B.B. Chang with his older but vibrant and excited uncle. The wiry snowy-haired man wore athletic spectacles with a sports band. They were both clad in identical running suits that were obviously expensive and very sharp.

"This is my Uncle Ishido," said B.B. proudly. "Ishido has raised my sister and I from our parents death." B.B. bowed slightly in respect to his uncle who returned the gesture. He is a long time member of the safari and my companion."

"Hello! I have heard a good deal about your work in Japan with

young people. I am so glad to finally meet you," said Weinberg bowing
to the Japanese man.

Ishido bowed slightly in return and smiled vigorously at the group,
revealing a mouthful of pearly white teeth.

"As they say in America, let the good times roll!" Ishido said as the
others laughed.

"He loves American rhythm and blues," said B.B. laughing along.

"B.B. King is my man!"

"Guess what he calls my sister?" B.B. asked. *"Lucille!"* he announced
as the group burst into laughter at the mention of B.B. King's legendary
red Gibson guitar.

Still chuckling, Weinberg introduced a short happy woman named
Rosa. Dressed in a bright yellow blouse and khaki slacks, she looked
like a vacationing tourist. Her makeup and long jet-black hair, pulled
through the opening at the back of her baseball cap into a ponytail,
looked perfect. She said hello to each member of the group and shook
their hands one at a time with a personal comment for each. Rosa was
obviously what you would call a "people-person!"

"Jim, it is so very nice to meet you!" she said to Jim. "Weinberg has
told me about you. You know, he is quite impressed with you. You must
be someone special!"

Jim blushed and shook her hand gratefully. Her soft flowing South
American accent were perfect companions for her graceful style.

"Now, where is my new little spark plug?" Rosa asked as she stood
on her tiptoes and tried to survey the camp.

"Oh, there she is."

Rosa pointed in the direction of a scuffle. There was a man trying to
help a young lady carry her pack and she was having none of it. As they

drew closer Jim could hear her arguing and protesting. Finally, she jerked the pack from his arms and broke it free. The pack flew through the air and landed at Rosa's feet, barely missing a ducking Weinberg.

The girl darted into the middle of the group, retrieved the pack, stood and pulled a white designer baseball cap off her light brown pony-tailed hair.

"Karin!" said Rosa with great concern. "Are you all right?"

"You bet, I just had to tell that sailor to shove off!" said the defiant Karin.

Jim rolled his eyes and turned away. There was something about the cocky girl that Jim could not tolerate. He made a mental note to have nothing to do with this irritating, in-your-face pest.

Weinberg patted Jim on the shoulder. Jim had not attempted to conceal his agitation.

"We all go along through this life at our own speed," he said patiently. "Perhaps there is a reason she is in our group, something she has to teach you."

Jim looked at his mentor in astonishment. "That," he thought, "was the dumbest thing Weinberg had said since he met him!"

"I have been many times into this forest," Gabriel addressed the other seven members of the group. "This part of Africa has not been inhabited by anyone for over a thousand years. Only the mysterious ruins of ancient ancestors hint at a time of settling long ago. There are only a few tiny villages there. You must be alert at all times."

Jim remembered the videos and lecture classes they had held both in America before departing and at the lake the last two days. The programs had been very well done and he had gained a great deal of confidence about the dangers and benefits of the plants and habitat in the jungle.

"Each of you, with your companion, will have one of the four Land Rovers as your base. It is equipped with all you will need for our journey," explained Gabriel, "Go now, and check your supplies and ready yourself for departure."

Jim was more than ready to hit the road. "Weinberg, which vehicle is ours?" he asked anxiously.

"Just over there," Weinberg nodded toward their Jeep.

Jim led the way and quickly began checking through their loaded supplies. Weinberg joined him and in no time they were seated and ready for the go ahead.

All around the bustle of activity was being repeated by the other groups of eight. Finally, a singing call went out in a local tribal tongue from one guide to another.

As if on cue, the sound of the birds, chimpanzees and the commotion of the cranking engines rose a decibel as if a crowd was cheering a sporting event from the grandstand. Jim bristled with excitement and gripped the handle at the open door of the Jeep tightly with both hands.

With Weinberg at the wheel, they fell in line behind the other three Land Rovers in their assembly led by Gabriel and Stephen. As they drove to the east the smooth tar road gave way to gravel.

They passed banana and rubber plantations on their way up and out of the valley. The expansive Miombo Woodlands opened up and swallowed the Jeeps. The trees, thick on each side of the man made road, reached up to brush the translucent sky, creating the effect of high walls about them. Because the road was still wide at this point, there was a large expanse of clear, blue sky to be seen over head. Birds circled and flew from one outcrop of giant hardwood trees to the other.

The trees began to meet together overhead as the road narrowed upon their exit from the encampment. It seemed to Jim that early morning soon became late afternoon since the trees blocked out so much of the bright sunlight. Refocusing for the filtered light, he could now see how matted and tangled the undergrowth was around each of the trees. So many large roots intertwining among an endless variety of plant shapes.

Jim looked up high. The chatter of chimpanzees that he had continually heard during his stay at the lake now had faces. Swinging throughout the maze of branches were dozens of all kinds and sizes of chimps and other smaller monkeys. Their shining eyes taking in the group's movement down the road with avid interest.

"So, Jim, what do you think now?" asked Weinberg with a little wink and a smile.

Jim smiled back, and took a deep breath. This was it. Here was the challenge to face the fears he had always felt but never spoke. The grandiose scenery, the wide neverending expanses he'd seen here in Africa, the powerful water flow he heard in the distance, and the sound of nature buzzing throughout this forest had transported him to another level.

He smiled to himself and took an even deeper breath, slowly exhaling as he slid down a bit in the in the seat. Tilting his hat to block out the bright sunlight, he was the man on the front of the brochure!

After they had been driving over an hour and a half, Stephen stood in the lead Jeep, waved, then called out to the others following to pull over to the side of the now dirt road. On Gabriel's orders they all got out of their Jeeps, took a stretch, and prepared a quick lunch.

It was clear that Gabriel, though young, was an absolute expert.

Stephen and he worked as a seamless team. They were not, however, robotic and stiff. They, too, were having fun! Joking with the group they made a rapid, but easy effort to get to know each one of the people in the team.

Jim thought, "How wonderful it must be to love your work!"

"We are well on our way to get to our arranged campsite by early evening. Our pace is just right," announced Gabriel smiling. At that they all climbed into their vehicles and continued up the sloping road.

Jim had switched seats with Weinberg. The afternoon lay before him in the shape of a winding dirt road. He steered the Jeep carefully as Weinberg kept him amused with stories of other safaris and tidbits of his family life.

His father had been an investment banker in Austria and his mother was an Englishwoman. She was a personal assistant for the president of a British bank doing business in eastern Europe. They had met at a business meeting where his father could not keep his eyes off the attractive prim and proper girl.

Although his father was Jewish and his mother was Catholic, they had fallen in love and moved to Austria. They were promptly tossed out of each other's church and synagogue for marrying outside the faith so they started attending a non-denominational Bible church.

"I grew up celebrating every holiday on the planet, from Shavuoth to Christmas!" kidded Weinberg.

Time flew as the two men talked and laughed together and pointed out the interesting sights.

As the shadows grew longer the Jeep chugged around a wide, slow bend. They all pulled their Jeeps off into the grass at the side of the road and sat and stared. No one spoke. Jim's mouth dropped open in astonishment as he sucked in a breath at the spectacle that lay before them.

Here was the highest point for miles around. With the sun at their backs the layers of the forest had cleared to give way to a glorious sunset sweeping across the canyon and rolling mountains beyond.

Jim had never experienced such a vastness of natural beauty, unobstructed and devoid of man's touch. It was so precious and pure. He felt as if he were a child seeing the sunset for the first time. Even Karin was silent.

Everyone felt their own quiet strength drawn from the dignity and power of the mighty natural wonder. Jim looked at each of them and caught himself wondering what they might be thinking. It was a new sensation to care about the others.

In a strange way he could feel himself becoming interconnected to this group of strangers. An invisible thread of common experience was knitting them together. They would remember each other for the rest of their lives.

As for himself, he couldn't help but think about how many sunsets like this he had missed, hunched over a computer or slugging it out in traffic trying to get home from the office.

He realized Weinberg, Stephen, and B.B were beginning to set up the camp. The sounds of the more experienced campers unloading the gear brought him and the other "green peas" back to the task. They all began excitedly lending a hand with a renewed vigor. What a camp site!

Before long their "Bush Motel," as they called it, was established and the fires were started for cooking the meal; and each one could take a moment to have time to themselves either in their tents or by wandering the plateau they had overtaken for the night.

Rosa and Karin were taking pictures of the birds and scenery. Rosa asked Karin to pose, which she finally agreed to do, after a lot of noisy protesting.

Jim heard Rosa say, "Honey, you are so pretty without that frown!" as she snapped a few photographs.

Jim knew she was trying to encourage the bitter girl. Karin smiled back awkwardly. She did not seem very comfortable with praise. Was there some experience that had turned this attractive person to anger?

B.B. and Ishido had a very expensive looking video camera and appeared to be in a high tech movie production. The two friends spoke rapidly in Japanese and were engrossed in the life of some insects at the base of a large rock.

Jim laughed to himself as he thought of the black and white Japanese movies he'd seen as a kid, featuring camera-tricked reptiles as gigantic monsters. Then he returned to help Weinberg and Stephen prepare the kitchen set up.

At dinner, everyone was bursting with chatter after their day of sequestered travel. Boisterous sharing of stories spawned amusing descriptions of other travels that created a warm and safe shelter from the largeness of their surroundings. Weariness finally crept up on the gathering. Gabriel made a paternal suggestion that they get some rest. Everyone was so full of the experience of starting their safari that they were buoyed by natural adrenaline, but each agreed and one by one they bid the others good night.

Jim walked up to the Jeeps to check one more time for anything he'd forgotten and was pleased to find his friend there. Weinberg's silhouette was framed by a basketful of stars spilled out across the forever blackness of the African night. He was smoking a pipe. The fragrance was sweet and aromatic. As it drifted into Jim's memory he recalled his father's pipe.

Silently, the two men looked up in wonder at forever.

Finally Weinberg spoke. "Why did you come, Jim?"

"Oh, I thought I would make sure I didn't leave anything out in the Jeep," Jim replied.

"No, not why did you come up here just now. Why did you come on the safari?"

Jim thought for a moment, then spoke slowly. "I'm not sure. You know I lost my job, already. I guess I didn't have much else going and thought it would be as good a time as any," Jim said looking down at his boots.

Weinberg pulled on his pipe. The glow of the tobacco coal lit his face in a dull amber light.

"Jim, I have been watching you. You seem uncertain. You are obviously a very smart and talented man. We both know you will find other work. Probably a better job, with more money. Right?"

"That's true," said Jim. Headhunters had been calling him for some time before this all came down. They were offering him some pretty tempting opportunities with other employers, but he had been afraid to venture out on his own."

"Then why are you here, instead of home putting your career back in gear?"

Jim wanted to go back to his tent but something made him stay.

"Weinberg, I feel like I am lost," he finally said. "I don't know what I want. I don't know what I feel. My wife says I am a louse and don't love her. I do, but I guess I don't show it. I can't seem to find the spark in life anymore," Jim's voice trailed off.

"Somewhere, somebody is doing something you love to do and getting paid to do it," Weinberg said.

"Yeah, they are in that tent right over there," Jim gestured toward the guide's tent.

"That is very well and fine if you are clear on what you love to do."

"Are you afraid?" asked Weinberg.

"Afraid of what?"

"You tell me."

Jim thought of the crippling fear that had haunted his every decision since childhood. How could Weinberg have nailed him so quickly?

"Maybe," he said, hedging. "Things have always been kind of laid out for me. This is all very scary. I can't even seem to size up my chances to win because I don't know what game I'm in anymore."

"What is the *real thing,* Jim?"

"What do you mean?"

"The real thing. What is the most important thing in your life, what is second, what is third?"

"I never thought about it. I guess my family, my health, my career…" he trailed off.

"If someone were observing your life and writing a story about you, what would *they* say are the most important? How could someone tell what was the real thing to you?"

Jim thought hard about the idea of someone given the task of describing his values by watching him go about his life. He wondered what was obvious.

Weinberg paused. "Have you read *The Three Treasures*?"

"Yes. Well, I have read the first treasure," he admitted, remembering he had told Benjamin he had read it all.

"Excellent!" said Weinberg. "That is the starting point for everything. You cannot make any decisions with clarity unless you unleash the power of your mind to change your world."

Jim listened closely.

"Have you ever thought about prioritizing your values?" Weinberg asked.

"Why?"

"Imagine two people with the same three values you just mentioned; family, career, health. The first person says here are my priorities, number one is family, number two is health and number three is career. The second person says career is first, health is second and family is third. Could you tell them apart?"

Jim thought, "Well, I guess, if the second person meant what he said then he would always choose his career over his family or health and so on."

"Exactly!" congratulated the teacher. "You could spot them a mile away!"

Jim thought about his priorities and where he actually spent his time.

Weinberg continued. "Think about this trip, for instance. What are the priorities for Stephen and Gabriel?"

"I didn't know there was going to be a test!" protested Jim, attempting a little humor. They both laughed easily.

"Okay, let me see, I guess their priorities would be safety, time frame, and then adventure, in that order," Jim was already beginning to see.

"Wonderful, Jim! That means their decisions would automatically be made based on these guidelines. Once the values are clear, the decision to take this road or that, where to camp and when to leave, are easily seen."

"Right, Jim!" encouraged Weinberg. "The Treasure of the Mind will help you gather wisdom, not more irrelevant data. Would you trade a life of meaning, joy, and understanding, for a trivial pursuit?"

Weinberg pulled on his pipe, exhaled slowly and blew a perfect little ring into the air.

"When I was in banking, and right up until recently, business success used to be about keeping up. Now things are accelerated, technology is exploding. You cannot keep up with everything. Now it is about making choices."

Jim saw that Weinberg was right. Just as Benjamin had warned him back in the office in America, he was like many other people whose only reference point was money and status. "It's a lot to consider, I know," said Weinberg, pulling on his pipe. "Begin the journey with your thinking process."

"My thinking process?"

"Yes, whether you realize it or not, you are already using a method to make decisions about the world around you. A series of filters you run against the data you take in. Call it your world view, the environment you were raised in or whatever, you have one and that is where you start."

Jim nodded.

"The starting point of the journey is to examine the ways of thinking you use now, *especially the ones that have ceased to serve you,* and separating reality from illusion."

"Illusions?"

"Let's talk about it tomorrow. Okay? We've got a big day ahead."

Jim thanked Weinberg for his insight and encouragement and headed for his tent. He re-read "The Treasure of the Mind" and made a few notes in his journal before twisting the lantern off. He lay flat out on his back, hands behind his head, and listened, safe in his cocoon, to the strange and wonderful sounds of a night in the jungle.

The River

"Hey, Jim! Is this awesome or what?" Andy stood on the narrow shaky dock and pointed down at a dozen brightly painted canoes. The groups had gathered back together for a special activity. "All right!" shouted Jim bounding out of the Jeep and heading toward his friend. Weinberg crossed the parking area toward the tin building to talk with the canoe trip operator.

"I used to canoe with my dad all the time. I love these things," said Jim as he reached Andy who was already sitting in a red canoe and flipping the paddle in an imaginary motion.

"Bom bom bom bom, bom bom bom bom," Andy mimicked Indian war drums and chanted as he carefully pretended to take slow strokes alternating on each side of the canoe.

"You are nuts, Andy," said Jim laughing.

"Ain't it great?" said Andy smiling. "I'm just having the time of my life. How 'bout you, Jim?"

"Yeah, I am having an excellent safari. Can you believe this country? It is so beautiful here. Everywhere you look is a postcard," replied Jim.

The busy river splashed against the muddy banks underneath the docks and disappeared into the swaying trees and patches of sunlight along the banks down river.

"Here we go!" called Weinberg easing down the steep incline to the river followed by Benjamin and the rest of both groups. He unfolded a black and white copied map and laid it out on the picnic table for everyone to see.

"We are right here," Benjamin pointed to a blue inked "X" on the map along the river. "We will follow the river downstream along this way." He slowly traced his sausage sized index finger along the blue line.

"The river has three major forks—it is very important that we take the forks as indicated on the map. Look for these blue signs along the way. They tell you're on the right part of the river. If you see red or yellow..."

"Stop and ask the traffic cop, politely!" called out Andy as the group laughed.

"Actually, you have two choices. You either pull your canoe out of the river and make your way up the bank back to the fork, or you continue on to the pickup zone for that tributary."

"Ya'll better be real careful if you decide to go down the red river way." The voice belonged to a tall American in his early 40s. The group turned around to face the dark tanned smiling face as he stepped up to the map.

The operator of the canoe trip was wearing a Safari Adventure Company baseball cap, khaki shorts, a blue denim shirt, and was carrying a large thermos.

"The reds will kick your butt if you don't know how to navigate the rapids." He cleared his throat, raised his eyebrows, and gave them his most challenging stare. "Take it easy as you approach the Ys and you will be okay."

"I have had a lot of experience canoeing rapids, how tough are they here?" asked Jim.

The canoe operator turned to face Jim, sizing him up and down as he removed his hat and scratched the side of his nearly bald head. "We have had a lot of rain this season," he began, looking up at the sky, "probably get a big storm in the next couple a days. The river is high and extra fast right now.

"How about the rocks in the rapids?"

The canoe operator, looked sternly at Jim then spoke in almost a whisper. "Listen, this river is more dangerous than it looks. It's real shallow here but there are some very deep parts."

He pulled his cap down and scratched the half dozen hairs left on his head and continued.

"I was fishing one of them deep holes about three months ago when I got a bite on the line so hard it pulled my rod and reel into the water. It was a new setup, rod and reel and all, and I guess I just acted without thinking. I jumped over the side of the boat to see what took my stuff." The large man was gesturing a dive and swimming action to support his story. The safari members, especially Andy and Rosa, were hanging on every word.

"The minute my eyes cleared the water I could see the culprit. It was a 10-foot shark! I had heard tales of them swimming up this river but never saw one before. Like I said, though, I just acted without thinking.

"The shark had my reel in its mouth so I just swam down to it and struck it on the nose, like they do in the movies. It released my rod and reel and I reached out and grabbed it."

"Oh, my!" whispered Rosa as the other members leaned in to hear the rest.

"Just as I grabbed the rod, the shark snapped down on my elbow and bit my arm right in two!" Now the canoe operator was wild eyed and waving his elbow as if to get the shark to release it.

Jim was totally immersed in the story up until this part. He saw Benjamin roll his eyes at Weinberg with a smile.

"Like I said, I wasn't thinking, just acting on instinct. Since I was all alone I just grabbed the hook and sewed my arm back on with fishing line and swam back up to the boat!" The storyteller stood defiantly with his hands on his hips as the group groaned at the whopper.

"Ask me how I'm doing now," he baited them.

"How are you doing now?" The group chanted loudly.

Without speaking, the grinning canoe man put one hand in a classic thumbs up sign, while the arm he claimed was bitten off, he turned a thumbs up sideways, his thumb pointing at the other hand.

"Ha-ha-ha!" howled Andy as the others began to get the joke, "he sewed it on wrong!"

"The main route is very safe and there ain't no sharks. I was just kidding! Come here, let me talk to you, though Hiawatha," he pointed at Jim.

Jim stepped aside with the operator as they walked a short distance from the group while Benjamin continued.

"With the river this high, you are over the top of a lot of the smaller stuff but it moves really fast so be extra careful," said the shark tale warrior. "If you have experience you will be okay, but keep your life vest on all the same."

"Thanks. That's a very funny story," said Jim with a smile.

"Thanks, I just warn the group because most folks don't need to be going down that way. They just want to have fun and see the jungle from the river, not floating down it, freaking out clinging to their vest! Is this your first trip with the Safari Adventure Company?"

"Yes it is."

"I would like to talk to you after your little journey. Give me a call or drop me a line and tell me how it went. Okay?" The smiling canoe operator handed Jim a slightly soggy business card.

"Sure, I would be glad to."

The pair shook hands and talked quietly as the rest of the safari members discussed the trip.

"The river empties into Lake Koana." Benjamin indicated the large body of water on the map for the group. "Whichever way you go—red, yellow, or green—you will reach the lake close to the same spot. Bear to your right across the lake and head for the pickup point here."

Rosa, Karin, B.B., Ishido, and the others busily laced up the life vests and made sure of their gear. The canoe operator passed out small plastic wrapped packages to each person. "Lunch today will consist of beef and chicken fajitas." He grinned as he distributed the treats. "Texas' finest!"

Jim steadied a dark blue canoe while Weinberg boarded and held the dock for him. They eased their canoe into the faster water just as Andy and Benjamin did.

"Ahoy!" shouted Andy and waved his paddle.

"Ahoy!" Jim, Benjamin, and Weinberg yelled loudly.

Hearing the shout, the others, some still getting into their canoes, raised their paddles and fists and shouted back, "Ahoy!" The armada was under way.

"We decided to go down the red river way," said Andy as they found the touch for controlling the long thin fiberglass boats.

"Oh, that is such a surprise," said Jim smiling. "So are Weinberg and I."

"All right! Race?" taunted Andy as Benjamin rolled his eyes good-naturedly.

"What have I gotten myself into?" pleaded Benjamin.

"Let's take it easy and stay with the group until the fork. Then we will split off and do our own thing," Weinberg suggested as they all nodded acceptance.

"I don't remember meetin' that canoe operator before, have you Weinberg?" asked Benjamin.

"No," he replied.

"I talked with him awhile about the rapids and stuff," said Jim. "He says he's been out here about five years. He writes adventure novels that teach people principles to take control of their lives."

"Really?" asked Benjamin.

"Yeah, he is writing one now about the Safari Adventure Company, he said."

"Did you get his name?" Weinberg asked.

"Yeah, it was a real funny name. Let's see." Jim pulled the tattered card from his shirt. "Oh yeah, his name was Butts. Rick Butts."

"What a dreadful name!" said Weinberg shaking his head.

"I'll say."

The group called good-bye to the operator who was waving and smiling. Jim gave him a wave back to which the grinning man in the Safari cap gave the double thumbs-up sign with one thumb sideways again, then gave a dialing gesture and hand to the ear for "call me."

Jim nodded and laughed with the same screwed up thumb sign as they disappeared around the bend into the jungle.

The Diamond
and the Bear

The morning passed peacefully on the river with conversation and observation of all the unique sights. Everyone except Karin seemed to be immersed in the trip. She complained loudly and tried to tell everyone how to row their canoes, mostly by telling them they were doing it all wrong. When they reached the first cross point Benjamin and Weinberg informed the group they were taking the red way and would see them all at the lake pickup point.

For several miles, the allegedly challenging route was calm. They passed a section of high cliff walls on the right side of the river. Peering up into the jagged rocks they could see caves and paths along the face. A myriad of different colors and sizes of birds flew in and out of these high caves. A family of red monkeys sat about 20 feet above them in the mouth of a small cave and watched the four men go by with solemn blinking eyes.

With the sun high overhead, they stopped for lunch. After the delicious fajitas, Weinberg passed out a tasty sweet candy for dessert.

"Weinberg," asked Benjamin as they washed it all down with

canteen water, "would you tell the diamond and the bear for these guys?"

"All right then, I had intended to share this idea with Jim today anyway after our conversation last evening."

Weinberg settled carefully against the bank, wiggling his shoulders to get comfortable and took a deep breath to begin. It was obvious that he was flattered and relished the role of tribal storyteller.

"Well, boys," he began, "one of the most powerful ideas I have learned in my life is the secret of the diamond and the bear."

Andy and Jim turned to face Weinberg.

"Everyone is motivated one of two ways. You are either motivated toward good things or away from bad things. So we instinctively make our way in the world by this method, despite the fact that we don't even realize it. The difference seems very subtle but it makes all the difference in the world in our stress and fear."

"Explain the difference," asked Andy.

"Benjamin has a great example. Benjamin, tell 'em how you see it."

"Well, I grew up very poor," the voice of the huge Australian began softly. "My dad left my mum early on, and we moved back to her home town near Perth. But we couldn't afford to live in the city. My mum worked as a secretary at the minimum salary, and tried to support two rowdy boys. My brother and I were pretty keen on the groceries, if you know what I mean!"

Andy and Jim smiled. Jim tried to imagine Benjamin as a broad-shouldered boy.

"We lived in Sandy Town," Benjamin continued. "Now, Sandy Town is not on any map. It is where poor folks live. We had an electric light bulb in the ceiling of most rooms. A potbellied stove in the kitchen, but no running water in the house except for a manual pump on the kitchen washboard by the sink."

"No running water?" mused Jim. "What about the bathroom?"

"We had an outhouse," Benjamin continued. "On Friday nights we would have bath night. We heated water on the stove in every pan we had and poured it into a galvanized tub on the kitchen floor by the potbellied wood burning stove. Then we each took two turns bathing—dirtiest kid last!"

They all laughed.

"Now, what Weinberg is saying is that this experience shapes our world view. My mum reinforced it by the words she used. Have you heard these sayings? I'm not made out of..."

"Money!" said Andy and Jim in unison.

"Money doesn't grow on..."

"Trees!"

"A penny saved is a penny..."

"Earned!"

"If you don't watch it we'll end up in the...."

"Poorhouse!" they shouted.

"Oh, you heard that one all the way up in America, did you?" Benjamin said with eyes wide and eyebrows raised.

They all nodded and laughed loudly.

"Now, gentlemen, seriously," Benjamin's bearded face grew wistful, "do you think this experience affected me as I grew up and became a man?"

"Sure."

"You bet."

They agreed, already thinking of their own choices.

"You see, I grew up busting my tail to be successful. I got into sales and was number one because I was so driven, when I started my own business I worked outrageous hours, neglecting my family, killing myself, because I thought that was what good fathers are supposed to do," he admitted and lowered his head.

"You see," Weinberg added, "just like a lot of people, Benjamin was highly motivated but for a sick reason. He was motivated to avoid bad things. I call this the bear.

"This unseen bear is the fear of something bad, real or imagined, happening to us. It is a powerful motivator and very sick because no matter how fast we run, how much we accomplish, the bear never goes away."

"We are always running," added Benjamin agreeing with a nod.

"A young girl takes a risk and gives her heart to a boy. Her first love. She shares herself, her feelings and emotions and one day he says, 'I think we ought to see other people.' She is devastated.

"So she builds a fortress, a high stone wall and a moat around her heart. Her fear, the bear, is to avoid ever being hurt again. The years go by and she is unreachable.

"Never again will she allow this to happen to her.

"Miserable and unhappy, perhaps she even marries but remains distant, never knowing that that same wall that keeps out disappointment, keeps out joy."

The group sat silent as they all thought about the fears in their past that motivated them to avoid negative consequences.

Andy spoke first. "Wow. That is the exact reason people fail in my line of work, sales. Fear of rejection. I know I have sat at my desk and been afraid to call the best prospects on my chicken list because I was afraid of being rejected."

"Everything we do to avoid the bear costs us something," Weinberg continued. "How many wonderful opportunities have we all missed because of a fear that is out of line with the facts of reality, because of a lack of faith in our beliefs, ourselves, and the people around us?"

"Well, that is fairly depressing," said Andy with a chuckle, "better tell us about the diamond before we all commit suicide."

"Yes," agreed Weinberg.

"The diamond represents the good things that could happen. The positive, the dream, the goal, the belief, the power that pulls and empowers us to healthy motivation."

"When we switch our focus from the bear to the diamond, everything changes. Instead of the sick fear that motivates most, we are transformed by the courage, energy and power to make something positive happen.

"The day I shifted my focus to what was truly valuable and began to pursue the higher good, everything changed for me. I have never been the same," Weinberg concluded.

"You mean like a million dollars?" asked Andy. "I heard that big financial goals are important."

"Not necessarily," warned Weinberg. "You must begin with your values and how you are truly wired up for happiness. For some, big financial goals are important. For others, it could be a cabin by a stream with a fly fishing rod."

"The important part is that the diamond is the good things. Good for everyone, they are right and pure, like the second treasure.

They all nodded knowingly. Jim nodded too and wished he'd read the second treasure.

"Listen, most people labor under the illusion that they need more information to solve their problems. What they really need is the courage and strength to do the things they already know they ought to, when they least feel like it! That is why the identification of and shift toward that diamond is the key to incredible results." Weinberg said.

"Get it?" asked Benjamin playfully.

"Got it!" they shouted, their voices echoing along the river.

"Good. Very good," said Benjamin confidently.

All eyes went to the beautiful river. They listened to the water splash down the stream and imagined they were all alone here.

Suddenly, a six foot crocodile shot out of the water on the bank and dragged a bird back into the river. The screeching echoed down the cliffs until the water stopped the sound.

Walking on
the Water

The red and blue canoes shot through the boiling water slicing and bucking like barebacks at the rodeo. Jim, Andy, Benjamin, and even Weinberg howled with laughter and screamed with mock terror as they threatened to capsize several times.

Finally, the water smoothed out and grew wide again, flowing easily into the lake. It appeared suddenly ahead and in a moment they were spilled out of the tight confines of the river and into the expanse of the African lake.

Andy, always competitive, was paddling the front of the canoe while Benjamin steered. They made their way quickly toward the pickup point in Andy's imaginary race while Jim and Weinberg took a leisurely pace.

As Andy's red head slowly pulled away Jim stopped to rest. Leaning back in the canoe he dipped his hand in the cool water and splashed a few handfuls on his face and neck.

"Weinberg," he began, "I really liked the idea of the diamond and the bear."

"Good. It is exactly what I wanted to talk to you about after last night."

"But, can you give me an example of how I can use it?"

"Well," Weinberg looked out across the lake, scanning the shoreline. He seemed to be considering whether or not to tell Jim what he was thinking.

"All right," he finally said. "This lake has caused me to think of an example I had not considered before. But I don't want to get you sidetracked by the nature of the story and miss the point."

"Tell me. I will try to focus," Jim offered eagerly.

"There is a meteorological condition that exists at the Eastern end of the Mediterranean Sea. As the sun goes down the cooler air collides with the hot desert air and pushes wind and storms toward the Jordan Valley. It happened just like that one day, 2000 years ago."

"Is this another Bible story?" Jim asked, slightly irritated.

"I told you."

"Okay." Jim lifted his hat from where he had it pulled over his eyes and looked right at Weinberg. "I'm sorry, please go ahead. I will focus on the principle."

"Jesus and his disciples were done for the day and he told them to get in the boat and cross over the Lake of Tiberius, or Sea of Galilee, as some called it. He told them he would meet them over on the other side later. There was one problem and the disciples saw it immediately."

"I have heard this story," said Jim. "There was only one boat left."

"Exactly," Weinberg agreed. "He told them not to worry about the details, but just to be obedient. Reluctantly they departed. Have you ever been to the Sea of Galilee, Jim?"

"No."

"Well, I have and it is not a little pond. It is a large inland sea, very deep and very wide across. The storm blew in and in the darkness, the sea threatened to drown them. They were crying and terrified when suddenly they see a figure walking across the waves."

Jim listened intently, honoring his agreement to do so.

"At first, the story tells us, the disciples thought it was a ghost and they were even more afraid thinking they were surely going to die. Then they realized it was actually Jesus, walking in the water.

"That's when Peter..." Weinberg chuckled and shook his head, "old Peter, how much that guy reminds me of me. Well, anyway, Peter hollers out to Jesus and asks if he can join him."

"There is a risk taker," said Jim.

"Jesus said come on and to the amazement of the disciples, Peter hops over the side and starts walking on the water, too, that's what the story says. Now, these religious paintings from the medieval times have these disciples all wrong. They show these gentle, wimps, with faraway looks and halos. I don't think they were like that at all," said Weinberg.

"What do you mean?" asked Jim sitting up a bit, now quite curious in the change of Weinberg's tone.

"They were rough and tough fisherman. James and John were nicknamed Boanarges which means sons of thunder." Weinberg grew more animated and began waving his hands. "You don't get a nickname like that by being a wimp. They were rowdy tough guys, probably loud and raucous. Peter jumped up at Jesus' arrest and tried to take on a whole army of soldiers, cutting one guy's ear off with a sword before Jesus told him to stop."

"So?"

"I'll just bet when Peter went over the side and started to do his thing, he was showing off, you know, dancing back and forth on the water and hollering, 'Hey guys, look at me! Look at me!' " Now Weinberg was waving from side to side and tapping with his feet rocking the canoe vigorously.

Jim grabbed the sides of the boat and held on wide-eyed.

Weinberg threw his head back and laughed at Jim's panic. "The story seems a little bit more real out here, doesn't it?"

Jim nodded, hoping his compliance would calm his companion.

"Whew, well, the main point of the story is what happened next. I have been paraphrasing up until now…"

"Obviously," kidded Jim.

"The Bible adds this curious commentary on what happened next. It says," Weinberg cleared his throat and spoke more softly, *'And seeing the wind, Peter grew afraid.'* "

Jim watched as Weinberg's eyes met his.

"You can't see the wind," said Jim simply.

"Exactly, Jim," Weinberg cocked his head sideways with a slight smile and nodded at his student. "What did he see?"

Jim thought for a moment, then spoke. "He saw the bear."

"Yes."

"He saw the waves, heard the sound, and begin to think about the bad things that could happen," Jim thought out loud, encouraged by Weinberg's affirmation. "When he did, the rest of the story tells us, he began to sink."

"Right. Very good. The moment he shifted his focus from the diamond, Jesus, the object of his courage, he began to focus on all the things that could go wrong. Now, in my view, this story primarily serves to tell us more about Jesus than about Peter," Weinberg shot a quick sideways glance at Jim, "but the principle is still there."

Jim lay back in the canoe and thought as the boat rocked gently in the water. The slight smell of fish drifted into his nostrils as the wind rippled the water across the boat. The puzzle was growing clearer as another piece was snapped into place.

"Weinberg?" asked Jim, still lying back in the boat with his hat covering his eyes.

"Yes."

"You don't really believe that actually happened, do you? I mean, it's a great story and the principle is very powerful but that is just a super-stitious story from ignorant people. Isn't it?"

"I believe it really happened, just like that," said Weinberg.

"I read an article that said that Jesus, who was a very smart guy, was actually walking on a thick growth of lily pads and fooled the people who saw him," reported Jim, now peeking with one eye from under his cap.

"It takes more faith to believe a stupid story like that then it does to believe the story just as the eyewitnesses told it," Weinberg stated bluntly.

Jim snorted, "I see your point."

Weinberg stretched and took a drink from his canteen. Jim could tell he was getting ready to say something so he waited.

Weinberg finally began. "A little girl was riding on a streetcar in Chicago back in the 1920s, reading her Bible and minding her own business. A skeptic came up and asked her, 'Little girl, you seem so pretty and smart, do you really believe every word in that Bible is true?'

" 'Yes, as a matter of fact, I do, every word.'

" 'Well then, tell me, how did Jonah stay alive for three days in the belly of that fish?' the man asked with a smug condescending tone.

"The little girl thought for a moment then replied, 'I don't know, when I get to heaven I'll ask him.'

" 'Well, what if you get to heaven and he's not there?' said the man, sensing he had won the debate. She looked up at him with clear blue eyes and said, 'Well then, *you ask him!*' "

The Real Real Jungle

There was a light and steady tapping noise in the tent. Jim slowly became aware of his surroundings and awoke to find that it was raining. The corner of the tent had a slight pull away from the border and little drops were slowly forming and falling every few seconds. Jim put his hand out to touch the water the way you touch a sore spot on your body for no reason.

He pulled on his pants and shoes and crawled out of the tent, tugging the wide brimmed hat down over his head. The rest of the camp was already gathered in the main cook tent and conversation was lively.

Karin was arguing with Stephen about the proper way to make oatmeal while the others looked on with amusement at her seriousness about such a trivial matter. They were all doing an excellent job of enduring her particular nature, so far.

Jim poured himself a cup of coffee, added some powdered cream and pulled a campstool next to Weinberg. His new old friend gave him a smile and a pat on the back.

"Top of the morning!" Weinberg said in a happy voice. "Nice weather we're having, huh?"

"Well, at least its not the monsoon," said Jim, commenting on the fact that although it was raining it was a gentle morning shower and not a downpour.

"Give it but a little time," said the guide to both Jim and the group. "The way of the rain in this valley is that the little brother rain comes first to announce his bigger brother is on the way! I fear that soon we will be experiencing much heavier weather. After breakfast I want us all to make some modifications to our campsite to prepare. You will notice I had already selected a high spot for your tents last night so you will need not move them. Let's make the Jeeps secure and relax or hike in the area. We will not be traveling today."

Jim remembered his conversation with Weinberg about the priorities of the two guides. It seemed they planned safety first. He looked over at Weinberg.

Weinberg smiled at Jim knowingly and said, "Let's get the camp secure, then I'd like to show you that surprise."

As the two men worked together to double-stake the tents and make the camp extra safe from the predicted storm, suddenly there was a scream. It came from the area where the two women's tents were pitched.

It was Karin. She had tried to pull a second line across the back of the tent and succeeded in collapsing the whole thing on top of herself and was kicking the entire mess and shouting. Jim tried to keep silent but they all laughed out loud at the sight.

"I wonder what form of wild animal could be caught in this trap?" said Stephen with mock seriousness as he untangled the mess. "Oh, my! It is a man-eating oatmeal expert!" he smiled broadly as Karin's red tight-lipped face appeared from the folds of the tent. They all laughed loudly at his joke and immediately Karin grinned bashfully and began to smile in spite of herself.

Weinberg asked Jim to gather his things for a hike and to meet him down by the Jeeps. "Bring your journal and copy of *The Three Treasures,* too, Jim."

Packing the little notebook he was using for a journal, Jim grew excited. He wondered what mysterious surprise Weinberg had planned. He returned from the tent and made his way down the slope where Weinberg was already packing some supplies.

"Let's take along something to eat and prepare to be gone for the day," said Weinberg as he handed Jim several containers and packets of food and a first aid kit.

"Take a look at this."

Weinberg handed Jim an interesting electronic device.

"What is this?"

"It is an electronic location finder. You see, it uses satellites in orbit around the earth to beam back our coordinates. Look, this is our exact location within a few feet. We can look this up on my map no matter where we are. There is absolutely no way we can get lost, even on the dark continent!" Weinberg beamed proudly at his high-tech toy.

"What would Stanley and Livingstone paid to have one of those?" kidded Jim admiring the amazing device. "I had no idea anything like that existed! Are you taking me into the wilderness?"

"You never know what you will run into out here. It is always best to prepare," he said with his thumbs up and wink.

It seemed to Jim that Weinberg was taking a lot of stuff for a day hike, but he shrugged it off as the kind of caution older people were known for. Jim was full of breakfast and more concerned with the load he would carry than the potential problems he may encounter. He remained silent, however, in deference to his new mentor.

They turned together and looked across the valley. The camp stood in a clearing on a slope about half way up the foothills that led to a large green mountain. Jim was used to seeing naked Rocky Mountains. The dense foliage that covered the rise ahead made the mountain look soft and plush in the distance.

Although the sun was hidden by the low clouds, it was still rather bright. The mist from the floor of the valley gave the entire scene a surreal look. This was really Africa! Shockingly green and vibrantly alive. Brightly colored birds of blue, red, and white called out from the bush and swooped from tree to tree. Their shrill voices echoed at different pitches from one end of the valley to the other.

Weinberg turned and pointed to a path that disappeared into the trees. They hiked ahead in intentional silence, absorbing the experience and turning their own private thoughts. For over an hour they made their way on the remarkably clear lane gently climbing ever upward. Jim took in the sights and sounds and became immersed in the beauty of the incredible forest.

The rain was very different here because of the thick trees. It would hit the canopy overhead then collect on the leaves like a bucket. When they were full the leaf would yield to the weight and spill huge drops with a loud "PLOP" onto the leaves and ground below. When one hit you it felt like someone pouring a cup. You could hear the sound of it everywhere but nowhere in particular as though it was up on the roof.

Occasionally they would come to a place where a hole would open up in the trees overhead. Jim removed his hat and the misting rain would softly drift onto his face. It was cool and refreshing at this higher elevation. He rubbed the pure water on his eyes and face roughly, feeling the natural stimulation and energy.

Weinberg stopped abruptly and put his hand back, placing it on Jim's chest. Jim was looking down, his mind a million miles away from alertness. He looked up and his heart jumped with surprise when he saw why Weinberg had stopped. The path had taken a sudden right turn. If Weinberg had not caught him, he would have gone right over a cliff!

They looked out together over a spectacular sight. There was a huge waterfall tumbling across the opposite side of the canyon. Its peaceful flow at the headwaters reminded Jim of the slow way a roller-coaster takes the last few yards before screaming down from the top.

The waterfall must have been over five hundred feet from the top down to the bottom where it exploded into chaos and spray in the rocks below. The jungle had thanked the river by growing a thick bank of bush, trees, vines, and flowers, bathed in the mist of the spray. Dozens of monkeys scampered and played in the trees, safe in this inaccessible place from predators.

From there you could see the river wind lazily on through the canyon for miles before disappearing again into the paws of the jungle. Just then the sun broke through the darkening clouds and shot an incredible rainbow across the entire scene. The two men basked in the intense clarity and color of the moment.

Jim's heart began to slowly return to normal as Weinberg spoke his first words since they began.

"There are some places on earth where the hand of God is clearly visible. This is mine, Jim."

Weinberg invited Jim to join him on a gigantic smooth rock that lay behind the path opposite the cliff. Jim sat his pack down and stretched out on the natural stone bench. He hadn't noticed how tired his legs were. It felt good to sit. They watched as the clouds reclaimed the little hole in the sky and the rainbow faded. Even when it was gone it seemed somehow indelibly etched in his memory.

Not wanting to rush the moment, Jim drank from his canteen and waited for Weinberg to speak.

"It has been seven years since I was here last. I feel ten bloody years younger right now because this place has not changed a fraction. It's funny but even the smell is the same. Have you ever noticed how a smell triggers a memory?" he wondered aloud.

Jim thought about the smell of grapes. When he was a boy his mother had taken him to his aunt's house where she and her sisters made homemade grape jelly. The smell of grapes being cooked and the paraffin his mother and his aunts had used to seal the tasty delight was fresh in his mind though it was almost 40 years ago. His aunt had died two years later and Jim had forever associated the sweet smelling memory with her face.

"I can recall sitting here with Colonel Featherwood over twenty years ago and smelling those flowers." Weinberg pointed to a large bush with brilliant white flowers, their sweet unique aroma permeated the place and settled into Jim's memory.

Jim leaned back on his pack and tried to drink it all in; the morning, the hike, the waterfall, the rainbow, the memories of his aunt and all the other memories that dominoed out of that one. First his gentle mother, then his stern father, came to him in words and stories viewed from the tender eyes of his childhood.

In his imagination, he looked down on the faces of his own children. Their childhood deeds and antics played like a movie in his thoughts. Soon his mind was miles away.

Opening his eyes, he tried to think of something to say back to Weinberg but there were no words in his vocabulary that would add a thing.

The rain had stopped. Weinberg pulled out his journal and began to write. Jim reached into his pack and found his copy of *The Three Treasures*. He opened it and began to read.

The Second Treasure

THE TREASURE OF THE HEART

If you have heeded the words and employed the lessons thus far, you have embarked on the journey to carefully gather the most valuable treasures of life. You are to be applauded! Most never take the first step! You now need to understand what we could not suggest at the first.

The treasure of the mind has given you tools and the information necessary to design a road map that will take you anywhere you choose to go. Up 'til now you have been in the process of gathering and focusing solely on your own lot. There is much more!

In order to begin to find the deeper fulfillment of life we must return to the universe everything we have gained thus far. It is a principle of unquestionable truth that the only key that will unlock the most profound levels of wisdom and joy is borne of self denial. This awesome treasure is only discovered at the giving of all for the benefit of others.

There is a river that winds gracefully through a most beautiful land. It is populated by abundant life on both sides. It is the source of water, indeed life, for untold numbers of people and creatures great and small. At the end of the journey the river runs into a very sad place.

You see, the river empties into a vast inland sea that has no outlet. Instead of the rich life that accompanies the river all along the way, the sea is desolate and bitter. In its waters travel no living thing whatsoever! Its shoreline is an alkaline wasteland with no living plant for miles and never the footprints of animals, for they cannot drink of it lest they die.

With no outlet it has become stagnant and poisonous. It takes in the best and devours it for itself and therefore it has earned, rightfully so, the name, The Dead Sea. This is the state of a person who takes and never returns to others. Thinking himself wise and successful he is instead the victim of his own greed and selfishness.

Contrast the loving giving person who seeks first to meet the needs of his fellows. His is a life of considerably more value than the former. He alone will know the joy of the smile of sincere appreciation, the warm caress of a thankful handshake, the embracing hug of gratitude of the one who has had an important need met.

Sadly, in our modern age there is an awful concept at work in the world at large. That is to think that if I give something away it is lost forever. Consider. If I give my time can I ever regain it? If I give my gold coins, my possessions, my attention, or honor, am I not required to go out and earn them again if I ever hope to be repaid? Though it seems so to the unsophisticated, the answer is a resounding NO!

In the fabric of the universe, all things given are retained in eternal time. Some are returned directly as our needs should call. Most reappear to us in the form of our own needs being met from an unpredictable source. This is the concept ancient scripture refers to as "Treasures in Heaven."

Here is the greatest miracle of all. When a person gives unselfishly to meet the needs of another he does not receive back the equal portion. He actually gets back substantially more than he ever gave in the first place! You may scoff here, and if you do, you are in the majority. The world has always laughed at wisdom. Only faith can witness the truth of this matter and only trust can attempt to find out. In the end all giving results in abundant return far beyond the original investment.

As we love and give to others we find our own deepest needs for self-esteem and power met and exceeded. As we turn and deprive our fellows of that which we could readily give, our real joy slips through our fingers into a Dead Sea.

We can hear your voice now saying "the books and learning were easy to find and read. How shall we learn of this treasure? Where shall we find the path to its possession?" The answer is at once both simple and hard.

First, you must know that this answer is found down a road called the Via Dolorosa. Second, that the doorway that leads to this road is entered from any point around you where the choice between selfishness and generosity is to be made. You are making the choice daily. Choose to be the giver, not taker of life.

"Do nothing from selfishness or empty conceit, but with humility of mind let each of you regard one another as more important than himself; do not merely look out for your own personal interests, but also for the interests of others."
— *Philippians 2:3 & 4.*

Jim folded the last page over to save his place and closed the book. It had never occurred to him that the old saying "it is better to give than receive," might really be true. "Maybe that is why it got to be an old saying!" he thought to himself.

The image of the time he gave Claire that bike she wanted so badly popped into his mind. He could still remember the wide joyful eyes of his little daughter when she saw it under the Christmas tree at 6:30 in the morning. Tracey and he had done an excellent job of telling her they could not afford it and doubting Santa's ability to get the handlebars down the chimney.

He could almost feel his hands around her tiny shoulders in the soft teddy bear pajamas. Her grateful, slender arms once again were squeezing his neck as she said "Oh, thank you, Ookies," her nickname for him, in that little girl voice. A lump came to his throat as he closed his eyes to better capture the forgotten moment.

For certain, he knew he got a lot more pleasure in giving to her than even she had gotten from receiving the gift.

He looked up and saw that Weinberg was no longer writing but staring directly at him.

"I was reading about the Treasure of the Heart," Jim said quietly.

"Yes, The Treasure of the Heart. If I had understood that five years before I did, I could have saved so much pain and sorrow in my marriage."

"How do you mean?" asked Jim.

"I played the king of fools in the early years of my marriage." Weinberg offered immediately. "Oh, I was quite the gentleman in the courting stage. Once she was mine, however, I treated her like property. When she was sad, I was angry, when she was angry I was mean, when she was lonely I was callous and uncaring.

"I always looked for what I could get from her. I always took and I only gave to get my way. I married her so she could solve my problems. It never occurred to me that I had a responsibility to be her soul mate." Weinberg looked away now across the canyon toward the waterfall.

"What happened?" asked Jim after a moment.

"I read *The Three Treasures*. I took the safari, just like you are doing. I listened to Featherwood until he was blue in the face and when I finally got it I went to her and begged her to forgive me," Weinberg offered candidly.

"And did she?" Jim asked.

"Absolutely not!" Weinberg said laughing. "After all the things I had said and done I hardly believed myself. Yes, she was rightfully skeptical but I determined to show her my newfound love was real. In the end, what we do speaks much louder than anything we say."

"How are things now?" Jim pressed.

"Well, that happened 25 years ago. She passed away two years back, Jim. Part of the reason I have come back to the safari this time is to fill the void that losing her has left in my life. To answer your question as it related to your own marriage I must tell you that we grew to love one another in the most profound way.

"Our relationship began to get real when I began to show her unconditional love. You see, Jim, in conflict resolution it is incumbent upon the stronger to initiate peace. The weaker cannot initiate the peace; it won't work. It was up to me to take the first step.

"I am very sorry that you have lost her, Weinberg. You must miss her very much," Jim offered softly.

"Yes, I miss her but I am absolutely certain I will see her again in a short time in heaven. We have an appointment to keep you know!" Weinberg smiled and gave his thumbs up. It was the kind of smile that you have to earn the hard way.

Jim thought about his own marriage and wondered if he were the strong one. Then a question came to mind from *The Three Treasures*.

"Weinberg, what is the Via Dolorosa?"

"The Via Dolorosa is 'The Way of Suffering.' It is the Latin name for the road that Jesus traveled from Pontius Pilate's court to Golgotha, The Place of the Skull, where he was crucified. It is symbolic for the path of self-denial and absolute sacrifice of one's own self for the good of others.

"That is incredible," whispered Jim. "I didn't know that."

"The verses from the Bible in the 'Treasure of the Heart' are actually followed by the words: 'Have this attitude in yourselves which was also in Christ Jesus, who, although He existed in the form of God, did not regard equality with God a thing to be grasped, but emptied Himself, taking the form of a bond-servant, and being made in the likeness of men. And being found in appearance as a man, He humbled Himself by becoming obedient to the point of death, even death on a cross.' "

"Are these the exact words?" asked Jim, amazed at the quotation.

"Yes, the exact words," replied Weinberg.

"How did you learn the exact words?" asked Jim again.

"Well, actually, I memorized them. It has really worked to transform my life by renewing my mind. The most powerful way I have found to feed my mind is with real truth! When I look at what Jesus did for me it is much easier to, in turn, do these much smaller kindnesses for others," said Weinberg."

Jim was lost for words. The ideas, the power of Weinberg's story, and the awesomeness of the location were data sensory overload for him. He turned toward the canyon and stared out across the sky. It had begun to rain again and the clouds were growing darker.

Jim leaned forward and strained his eyes to verify a curious sight. There was a Jeep far away across the canyon on the other side of the river moving along a dirt road. It was only there for a moment, then it disappeared silently around a turn and back into the jungle. Looking more closely he realized there was a clearing at the base of the falls on the other side and a winding path that went all the way to the top.

Jim traced the steep path in his mind and made a note to himself to ask Weinberg if it would be possible to hike up there. It would wonderful to view this compelling place from the top of the waterfall.

In a little while, Weinberg suggested they eat some lunch. Jim checked his watch and realized they had been gone over three hours. He was feeling quite hungry. The food tasted marvelous.

"So, this is what you wanted to show me?" asked Jim.

"No," smiled Weinberg, gathering up his things, "I am going to show you something very few living people have, or will ever see. Let's go."

The Ancient Adventurers

The narrow road along the canyon wound back into thick trees and became almost invisible. There were a few places where the underbrush had begun to take back the trail. Broken branches and fresh machete marks told them someone had recently been through here. The going was mostly easy.

They hiked and cleared, crossed a small stream, and finally came to a wide-open meadow. Weinberg pointed to a hill off to the left and said, "Over that hill is the second place I wanted you to see today." He then headed off toward the hill at a quicker pace. Jim hurried to keep up with the obviously excited Weinberg.

"He must be eager to see whatever it is," thought Jim. "He hasn't moved this fast since we left!"

Covering the short distance to the crest of the brushy hill they reached the top together. Jim stared in astonishment.

There in the middle of the vast African wilderness sat what appeared to be a European monastery! Its unmistakable bell tower and spire rose up from the rich green valley. The walls and out-buildings were very much intact although the grass and growth around the structure told the tale that there were no inhabitants.

Weinberg hesitated for only a moment to view the monastery from the hill and then began to make his way down the back of the hill and towards the building. Jim looked at Weinberg, looked at the monastery and slowly began to follow.

Approaching the building from the rear they made their way around to the front. The courtyard was visible through the place in the wall where some great wooden doors must have once hung. Instantly, Jim was struck with an overpowering sense of the power of ancient history. He rubbed the goose bumps from his forearms as he walked across the stone courtyard toward a well and a stone bench in the center of the yard.

Although the monastery had been neglected for many years there was a peaceful feeling of its unshakable consistency that seemed to say, "I am here and nothing can make me go away!"

"What in the world is this place doing way out here?" began Jim.

"If these old walls could speak…" Weinberg began and then paused, "It is just incredible, isn't it Jim?"

"Tell me about it, Weinberg," Jim asked.

"Featherwood came upon this place right after World War II while on a safari with the club. In those days they really roughed it, you know, on foot with dozens of bearers and everyone carrying large amounts of gear. They explored and took photographs, quite dangerous really.

"Anyway, Featherwood had heard tales of a group of monks from northern Africa in the second century who had ventured deep into the sub-continent as missionaries and had actually established a monastery south of the Congo River basin. When Featherwood came across this place he was thrilled. He actually made several trips here and brought some highly qualified people in to study it.

"Featherwood brought me here on my first safari and I saw the waterfall and this place all on the same day just as I am showing it to you. He told me what he believed to be true to the best of his research."

Jim sat spellbound and listened.

"It seems that a man named Justinius, who was a disciple of Andrew, one of the twelve disciples of Jesus himself, grew discontent with the selfish way the monks in North Africa and Europe had withdrawn to monasteries. He believed they were hiding far from anyone who did not believe 'The Way' as Christianity was called in those days.

"He went to Antioch, Constantinople, and Rome to seek the people who were considered the higher-ups of his faith and was very disappointed in the hindrances put on his brothers by their entanglement in the politics of the day. Stuck between the worldly cities and the reclusive monks, he gathered a group of followers and headed south to reach the people he had never seen with the good news of his faith."

"That is absolutely incredible!" said Jim in amazement. He had always been fascinated with stories like this. What courage these men had. What conviction! Jim had dreamed of being an archaeologist as a young boy staring at *National Geographic* magazines. Maybe it was this fascination which what had first attracted him to the safari?

"The fact that he was not killed is the greatest miracle! He had to cross the territory of cannibals and savages. In fact, this very land was inhabited by some of the fiercest tribes up until recent times."

They sat at the fountain and looked around at the painstaking construction that seemed so out of place in this land. The stones, Weinberg explained were hauled from the ruins of an ancient African city about a mile and a half away. The ruins were over 1000 years B.C and made a convenient quarry. The monks fashioned them to resemble the familiar European counterpart. The result was odd-sized and rough which made for a wild and natural look that Jim thought was at once strange and beautiful. The work that must have gone into this place was incredible. Weinberg said it had taken almost ten years to complete.

After they had rested, Weinberg suggested they take a look around. They crossed the courtyard and entered a door at the side that led into the monks living quarters. Weinberg produced a flashlight from his backpack and led the way.

The monks had built small simple cells. They also developed an ingenious ventilation system. It was remarkably cool and comfortable despite the African heat and humidity. Along the wall where a small writing table must have been sharp angular letters were carved in the stone.

"The monks were given to writing a favorite scripture in their rooms. Usually a 'life verse' or a special scripture that meant something unique to them," said Weinberg.

"I guessed they weren't writing graffiti!" said Jim playfully. He was having a wonderful time and felt like a great archaeologist. What a privilege it was to actually see and touch something so few would ever experience.

"Look here, Jim," said Weinberg shining his flashlight on some other writing above the Latin inscription. "Featherwood translated and wrote the words in English."

Jim looked down to see the words, "I can do all things through Christ who strengthens me," written in black above the carefully chiseled Latin verses.

They made their way along the halls and entered the chapel. Jim drew a quick breath of surprise as he looked up at the large two story room. The monks had constructed a stunning primitive church here in this desolate place. The short railing in front of the platform was made from highly polished dark brown stone.

The walls were drawn with pictures of Bible stories from the Old and New Testament times. The colors had faded but still you could clearly see the images of angry Moses parting the sea, Daniel patiently praying in the den of lions, and the gentle Christ on his knees washing the feet of his astonished disciples.

A sculptured statue of Jesus on the cross surveyed the room from high above and behind the stone pulpit. The stone benches were lined in little rows. The place must have been able to seat almost 100 people. Weinberg sat on the back row and silently looked around, as if admiring an old friend. Jim sat reverently beside him. They looked like two church visitors who had arrived early and were waiting for services to begin.

All at once the dim room exploded in a rainbow of bright colored light! There were streams of sapphire blue, ruby red, gold and emerald coming in from all around piercing the thick stone walls.

"The natives brought quartz pieces to the monks as gifts when they first arrived," Weinberg explained, chuckling at the expression on his astonished companion's face.

"When they began to build the chapel, the monks inserted them in the walls and found quite by surprise that sunlight pierced them in a stained glass effect. The monks had always planned to light it with candles. Since the Monastery has its back to the West, this chapel literally glows in the afternoon sunlight."

"This is extraordinary, Weinberg. How many times can you say 'Wow!'?" asked Jim, looking around. "Why are there so many seats for a handful of monks?"

"Well, the monks were not here to hide from the world. They came to teach 'The Way' to the people. There were many converts and in a few years the chapel could not hold them all at the same time," said Weinberg. "This was actually quite a bustling community in its day."

"How did Featherwood learn so much about the group?" asked Jim. "There is not that much information on these walls."

"Featherwood was quite the amateur archaeologist. He excavated and uncovered records in a trash heap nearby. His greatest prize, he told me was how he found part of the journal of Justinius while digging through a separate section a short distance from the monastery. That is where he learned much of what we know today. It is in a lovely antique glass display case back at the lodge where we met," said Weinberg.

"I believe," he continued, "this is a living example of the Via Dolorosa. These men gave their lives to serve others. They abandoned everything familiar for a cause higher than themselves. What joy they must have known! What incredibly valuable lives they lived!"

The light faded as the sun ducked back behind a cloud reminding the men they had an hour and a half hike back to the camp. So they reluctantly gathered their things and prepared to leave. They turned to cross the front of the chapel when Jim tripped and fell face first across a coffin shaped wooden crate.

He sat on the floor and rubbed his shin, glaring at the offending box. It was pried open and the barrel of a gun and the stock and sight of another were easily visible through the opening. It was in this dimming room that he noticed an assortment of ivory tusks strewn among the boxes across the front of the chapel.

"The monastery is being used by poachers," said Weinberg sadly. "Let's get out of here, we have a long way to go to get back to the camp."

As they crossed the courtyard by the fountain near the entrance, they both heard the sound of a Jeep, gunning the engine. Jim peered around the wall and saw a band of five fierce-looking men wearing dirty military style camouflage fatigues and carrying weapons. They were arguing excitedly and heading straight for the monastery. Weinberg motioned Jim back in the chapel.

"They must have a road cut back to a village somewhere. There is no way for us to make it across the clearing and head up the path to camp without being seen," he whispered. "Let's circle to the monks' cells and I will show you a place where we can slip out the back and into the bush. Follow me!"

Running back into the monastery they moved quickly and quietly along the darkening corridor and exited through a narrow passageway into the dense jungle along the side of the monastery. The sound of the men arguing in heavily accented English grew louder.

Apparently, one of the men was very unhappy with the other over some matter of money. They were using the most vulgar language to describe what they would do to each other if the issue was not settled to their satisfaction. The other men were laughing at the fight and egging the two combatants on.

Jim and Weinberg found it very tough going in the growth around the back of the monastery. They were trying to be quiet yet make progress towards the path back to the camp. The poachers disappeared inside the chapel and the whole area became eerily silent.

Weinberg turned to Jim and said, "We are going to have to try to get back to camp before dark. Gabriel knows where I have taken you. If we do not return, he will set out after us in the morning and he might run into these miserable fellows. I cannot run as fast as you, but I can make pretty good time. Let's make a dash across the clearing now and try to get over the hill before we're seen!"

"Let's do it," said Jim, his pulse racing at the danger and excitement. He did not understand the gravity of the situation, but was frightened at the unknown and ready to get back to camp.

"Do you have your pistol, Jim?" asked Weinberg.

"Sure I do," said Jim warily. Turning to Weinberg with a concerned look on his face he said, "I can't shoot anyone, you can't be serious."

Weinberg stared back at Jim silently.

"It's in my backpack," Jim answered the unasked question as he fetched the gun and slipped it in his belt.

The instant they stepped out of the underbrush, but before they could run, the entire band of men came around the back of the monastery and into the clearing. Jim and Weinberg lurched to a halt and backed quickly into the bush unseen. There they crouched just inside the foliage and watched as the men built a brush pile for a bonfire.

The poachers were drinking whiskey and laughing as they prepared for some kind of African barbecue. Jim and Weinberg were trapped between the wall of the monastery and the thick jungle. If they tried to work their way into the jungle the noise and motion in the thick underbrush would give away their presence. They could only sit helplessly and watch as the poachers lit the bonfire and drank as darkness fell.

A Long
Short Night

The two men silently shared the rations Weinberg had so wisely brought along. They talked quietly between themselves and although they were in a tough spot it was not all that impossible.

The plan was to wait until darkness when the poachers went to sleep. They could then steal across the camp and make some progress up the path, then high tail it back to camp at dawn. Surely the drunken poachers were not early risers. They lay back against a tree and waited for the darkness.

Hours later, Jim awoke to the sound of furious screaming. Weinberg and he had fallen asleep. Night had come. The bonfire was giving off a macabre orange glow to the scene before them.

The two men who had argued earlier were now face to face, quite intoxicated and literally shrieking at each other. They had rediscovered the unsettled money question and were threatening bloody murder if not made whole. The taller man was brandishing a machete while the shorter one was trying in vain to spit on him. Both men were wobbly, slurring their words, and hopelessly drunk.

Jim looked out at the scene before him in disbelief. Still sleepy, he felt like he was dreaming. He was in the African jungle hiding from outlaws. Their shadows leaped across the monastery wall in giant caricatures of villains amplified by the flickering firelight. If he and Weinberg were discovered, who knows what might become of them.

Suddenly, the man with the machete lunged forward. He swung the blade towards the throat of the spitter. Had he been sober he would have severed the man's head. Instead he raked him across the chest with a striking blow.

No sooner had the machete made its pass, when three gunshots cracked out. Their sharp clapping echoed into the jungle. The man with the machete jerked violently and fell back into the fire but not before pulling out a revolver and firing helplessly at no one. One of the bullets streaked into the jungle just past Jim's ear as he and Weinberg buried themselves in the dirt.

The machete man's body twisted in the fire in a sickening way as he died. The bullets in his belt began exploding at random propelling his assassins for cover. This they found absolutely hilarious and squealed with bizarre laughter at the fireworks show. They found joy in killing their own companion!

Eventually, the explosions ceased and the body settled, slowly undulating into the ashes. The poachers tended to their wounded friend and laughed and drank some more. Apparently, the machete man was not much liked by the group and was good riddance. They settled down and proceeded to get seriously drunk.

Weinberg and Jim had no opportunity to escape. Tired as they were, they drifted in and out of consciousness as the bandits randomly sang and fired their guns into the jungle like cattle rustlers. Eventually, the entire group collapsed on the ground and began snoring loudly.

After waiting to be sure the poachers were unconscious, Jim pulled Weinberg up from his spot. The older man had gotten sore and cramped in hiding. They crept quietly past the murderers, carefully averting their eyes from the smoldering cremation fire and disappeared over the hill just as the sky began to promise morning.

African Storm

Though it had rained steadily off and on all through the previous day, it had never really stormed as the guide had predicted. The men proceeded hurriedly back to the camp with the sound of thunder and occasional streaks of lightning punctuating their steady footsteps.

"Gabriel will be on the path looking for us right now. We are so lucky to get out of there before he got to the monastery. He might have stumbled right on top of that crew," said Weinberg looking up at the threatening sky. "How disappointing to find the old church being home to such a wretched lot!"

They paused for only a short moment to catch their breath at the stone bench atop the waterfall view. Jim could feel the energy of the black boiling clouds pushing up the valley in the high wind. Filled with lightning and peals of thunder as they advanced toward the hikers, they looked like a chariot of some mighty mythological warrior. Jim thought how easily the ancient and uneducated could be impressed to invent legends to explain such a powerful display of nature.

"Why didn't we take everyone along to see the monastery?" Jim asked a question he had pondered but hadn't had time to ask.

"Gabriel and Stephen were going to bring them up tomorrow." Weinberg replied. "They were exploring another area yesterday and I asked if we could come up here alone. Old time's sake, you know." Weinberg pulled his electronic location finder out of his backpack. It was smashed and useless.

"I must have crushed it sometime during the ducking and hiding," he said looking down at it sadly. "Nevertheless, I know this path very well, we won't be needing this fancy compass anyway," he said tucking the useless box back in his pack.

The storm was progressing and Gabriel would be searching for them along the way so they pushed on back toward the camp. Weinberg was strong. Despite the lack of sleep and stress of the terrible night before, the men moved with energy and purpose.

Jim's mind began to wander as they wound along the path. He remembered the day he found the Safari advertisement in his desk drawer and thought it was probably a bunch of old men in fatigues drinking cocktails and sleeping in campers. He laughed in spite of himself. Would he have gone if he had known about the danger of last night?

They drew closer to camp and still no Gabriel. Weinberg thought it odd and said so. Perhaps there was a more alarming problem. He couldn't imagine what. There were very strict guidelines of protocol for missing hikers.

At once, the jungle opened up and they could clearly see the path down to the Jeeps ahead. Weinberg stopped, then backed up a couple of steps. Jim stood beside him and looked down the hill in horror. There was only one Jeep and it had been set on fire and was now smoldering and destroyed! Farther across the clearing lay the destruction of the campsite. It was ransacked. Supplies, tents, and pieces of clothing were scattering in the rising wind.

"Weinberg, what is going on?" asked Jim

"Something is terribly wrong here, Jim," said Weinberg, his jaw set as he headed down hill.

Jim was the first to see the bullet casings near the campfire. Weinberg found the body. Gabriel had been shot several times. His cold body had been dead for hours.

They called out for the others and searched the area all around the camp, but no one answered. There were footprints on the Jeep trail that led off in the direction that they would have continued the safari. It appeared as though the others had gone ahead on foot. They found some of the supplies and parts of the tents scattered around in the bush. As they gathered what was salvageable, they shouted over the noise of the wind.

"Do you think the poachers did this?" asked Jim.

"Why in God's name would someone have to kill like this to protect their illegal turf," said Weinberg answering his question. "They must be trying to scare off visitors to the area."

"What about the local game wardens? How can they get away with this?"

"The odds of whoever did this ever being caught are very slim. You saw last night the world these people live in. They are more likely to kill the game wardens than be arrested and brought to trial!" Weinberg replied.

Lightning streaked across the sky and the wind threw the leaves into a shiver. Jim grabbed hold of his hat as the rain began again this time with larger and heavier drops. The storm Gabriel had predicted was coming and it was going to be big.

The men decided not to remain there for fear of the return of the poachers. They struggled down the Jeep road until the rain and wind drove them deep into the jungle. There, wedged between two large trees, they pulled a piece of tent over their weary bodies and heavy packs and huddled down to ride it out. The crude tent was dry and dark. Hidden from the road, they lay back against their packs and fell asleep as the sound of the storm droned on into another night.

Hopelessly Lost

Mountain peaks bathed in a golden-pink sunset descending into a lush emerald forest. Colored birds and flora abounded. Ruby and sapphire light from crystal gems imbedded in an ancient chapel wall. Greedy and vile men drinking, fighting, and shooting guns in the firelight. Jim sat down in the grass. His hand touched something warm and wet. A crimson stain of blood wept slowly off his outstretched fingers onto the body below. Body? Body!

Jolted from a nightmare, Jim bolted upright. Trying to stand, he caught his arm on the rope, which had been strung from the trees to create a makeshift lean-to for the night. Totally disoriented he stumbled, and fell backward onto the ground landing right on top of Weinberg.

"Jim, what in heaven's name are you doing?" cried Weinberg.

"Oh, man!" Jim shouted apologetically as the last twenty four hours tumbled back into reality.

"Here! Here! Jim, settle down now. It's okay, we're all right," said Weinberg, rubbing his ribs.

"Gosh, I'm sorry. Are you hurt?" asked Jim, as he scrambled to his feet.

"No. I'm fine. You do make an interesting alarm clock though!" He rolled over, sat up and gave his thumbs up sign.

Jim patted his new mentor on the shoulder squeezing an apology and appreciation. Jim was never one to show affection, but it came spontaneously. Weinberg put his hand on Jim's and patted a quick acceptance.

"Here, have a bit of breakfast," Weinberg handed him some dried fruit.

"Yeah…good idea. Do you have any bacon and eggs in there?" Jim asked, smiling weakly.

Jim put some of the fruit in his mouth and began to think about their next move. The fruit tasted sweet. Jim recalled how Weinberg loaded them up with supplies and how he had almost foolishly balked at taking the extra weight.

"Okay, Jim, what do you say we hike back toward the campsite and see what supplies are left. We'll use the sun as our guide during the day. That is, when we can see it." Weinberg looked up at the heavy foliage.

"We don't know where everyone else disappeared. Maybe we'll run across them later. More importantly, we have to be on the lookout for those poachers. We'll keep to the road but we'll have to be ready to bail into the forest if we hear Jeeps. It's just too risky to strike out through the jungle."

"Right," said Jim as he busied himself with the task. "You're right, let's get started. Best thing to do now."

It was taking longer than they thought it would to find the road. It soon became obvious they had cut their way deeper into the bush than they realized. Perhaps they were all turned around. Maybe they were not heading back to the road at all, but farther into the jungle. Jim began to worry.

After several hours it became crystal-clear. Neither man needed to say a word. They were utterly lost. Weinberg never showed any signs of fear or worry. He had maintained a positive attitude and reassured Jim they would find one of the roads soon. He encouraged him to press on and keep his eyes open. As they sat on a log by a small stream Weinberg bowed his head and folded his hands. Jim knew he was praying.

"I hope he throws one in for me!" thought Jim.

Finally, Weinberg looked up. His eyes were moist with tears.

"Weinberg, are you scared?" asked Jim, a little surprised.

"No," laughed Weinberg, wiping his eyes with his blue bandanna, "I just had the strongest impression of my wife. I felt as if I heard her voice. It was strange how the sensation was so real. She was saying not to worry. She was always such a great encourager to me whenever I faced a tough challenge. I guess I just got a little emotional. Happy, though!" He smiled and gave a little thumbs-up and winked a reddened eye.

Their spirits lifted when they saw a familiar looking hill through the trees. They decided to press on toward it. The struggle through the undergrowth had begun to take a toll on Weinberg and his weariness showed. With the next swing of his machete, exhaustion overtook him and it slipped out of his hand and flew into the air. Jim watched as the machete fell into the shallow ravine they had been walking along.

"Let me go down and get it for you," Jim insisted.

Slipping the backpack off his shoulders, Jim began to lower himself carefully down the side of the ravine. Sighting the machete with its handle sticking out from a bush a few feet away, he quickly grabbed it and started back up the incline.

As he looked up to get his grip on another vine, his eyes locked with those of an enormous black panther! It was poised and ready for attack, halfway between Jim and the top of the embankment. The muscular onyx body and the intense concentration in the panther's gleaming stare froze Jim in his tracks.

The hair on his arms and neck stood on end. He thought he was afraid of snakes but this was a million times worse. The green eyes of the huge cat were hypnotic as it stood silent just a few yards away.

Down the hill Weinberg's voice came softly. "Jim, just stand still. Don't move," he whispered hoarsely.

Jim's nightmare came to life as a blue and orange parrot flew noisily out of the trees just above the panther's head. The panther, startled, sprang sideways enough for Weinberg's carefully calculated pistol shot to miss the cat and shatter bark from the tree beside it.

Without waiting, Weinberg came crashing down the hill, shouting to draw the panther's attention onto him. It worked. The panther turned from Jim and toward the attacker. Weinberg came half running, half sliding, down the hill directly between Jim and the panther, shouting and firing the pistol as he came.

In instant reflex the panther unleashed a soul-wrenching scream, crouched and sprang at its attacker. The weight of the great cat drove Weinberg to the ground. He continued to fire the pistol into its belly, as the vicious killer tore at his face and throat with both spiked claws.

Jim ran to the brawl. With a guttural cry, he slammed the machete with all his might onto the panther's neck. Blood shot everywhere as the blow shattered the cat's shoulder bone. The wounded panther, still astride Weinberg, spun around and swiped at Jim, teeth bared and hissing. The razor-sharp claws ripped across Jim's chest and knocked him down the ravine again.

Instinctively, returning to its work, the still-powerful creature sunk its huge fangs into the neck of it's victim, choking off Weinberg's scream. The only sound was the "click-click-click" of the empty revolver as Weinberg continued to helplessly squeeze the trigger. In one great violent twist the panther shook Weinberg's neck like it had done so many times before to antelope victims.

Jim, scrambled back up the hill, and drew his pistol. In a leap he was only a few feet from the mauling terror. He raised the pistol and fired. The bullet ripped into the black fur of the panther's neck just above the machete wound. The frenzied panther unable to walk from a broken shoulder and already carrying several of Weinberg's bullets, instinctively tried to rush Jim. It began crawling toward Jim, the object of its searing pain, blood frothing from its gaping mouth.

Jim deliberately fired one shot...two shots into the killer's brain. As the second round slammed into its skull, the panther rolled over, clawing the air.

Weinberg's body had rolled under a bush. Jim pulled the bush aside and, lifting a blood-soaked wrist, tried to feel for a pulse.

Panic, anger, and fear took turns sending electric jolts into Jim's solar plexus in shock waves. In a white-hot anger he looked back at the dying panther, re-loaded the gun and fired every round into the now still beast.

He returned to Weinberg and knelt gently by his friend, stunned by the absolute brevity of their relationship. There was no good-bye. No last words to treasure. Should he bury him? How? He had no shovel!

The jungle had gone wild during the gunshots and the fight. Now the screaming birds and monkeys once so loud and raucous became very still. Eerily feeling eyes on his back, Jim turned slowly and saw another panther, glaring at him from behind a log just a few yards away!

Jim backed himself awkwardly down the ravine. Stumbling on a limb he fell to the bottom of the ridge. In shock and for fear for his life, he jumped up and ran as fast as he could.

Falling, running, falling, he tore through the bush until he thought his heart would burst. He finally collapsed. Up in only a moment, he ran again until exhaustion overtook him. He let himself roll to the ground and crawled helplessly under a huge fern.

In the growing darkness and seclusion of the foliage, he struggled to maintain consciousness. Pain seared through every inch of his tortured body. The terrible stinging cut from the panther's clawing, forgotten as he ran, now sliced across his chest in waves. The bruises and cuts from falling and being slashed by the jungle demanded relief. But, there was no relief.

Hoping against hope that the other panther would not track him, but unable to move on, Jim lay panting under the great bush like a doomed rabbit. Darkness swept across the jungle as he pulled the leaves across his body, curled up in a ball, and closed his eyes.

Beyond the Edge

During the night, an army of ants had found the leftover dried fruit in Jim's shirt pocket. He awoke in a panic to brush their trail off his neck. He hated and cursed the ants in the clear light of the dawn. He was hungry, too.

He forced himself to make a decision and take action. He could not lie here and wait for help or death! He couldn't allow himself to think about Weinberg, not yet. Swallowing hard he came out from under the waxy green fern and looked around.

He wasn't sure what time of day it was, only that it was daytime by the amount of light diffusing through the trees. He thought about eating the fruit ants and all, but brushed them away first and nibbled carefully at the morsel.

Calmer and rested, he knew he must go back to the top of the ravine and retrieve his backpack of supplies. He would have to overcome the idea of what he would find there in order to survive.

Following the broken limbs of yesterday's flight Jim proceeded cautiously, the small revolver drawn and ready. Making his way up the bank he recognized the ravine where the battle had taken place. Peering cautiously over the embankment, Jim saw no sign of Weinberg or, thankfully, the slain panther. The jungle had removed them. Relieved, yet lonelier than ever he searched for the backpacks. The lost machete lay a few yards away.

The scene appeared different than it had in Jim's imagination. The grass and bush was trampled down all around the blood stained ground. Broken branches and bent grass led away from the area into the jungle. "It looked as if an army had passed through here," thought Jim.

Jim's bright blue canvas backpack was right where he had laid it yesterday. Weinberg's dark red pack was lying halfway down the ravine. The lightweight aluminum frame was badly bent either by Weinberg's fall or the rushing panther. Jim ran his fingers over the bend gently, feeling the loss of his mentor. Looking inside the pack he saw some packets of food and a small worn Bible. Jim tucked them in his pocket without thinking, grabbed his own gear, and took cover between a grouping of tree trunks to think.

"What in the world am I going to do?" he said out loud, listening nervously to the smallness of his own desperate voice. The smell of the jungle, so humid and musty from the rain, mingled with the flowers and animal musk that permeated everything. His mind was silent and empty. As he sat between the huge, gnarled tree roots he began to differentiate between the noises from the forest. They had been blended before into a dull sameness. He listened.

Rustling foliage from small burrowing animals, chimpanzee laughter, and a symphony of bird calls greeting the morning came to his ears one at a time. As he raised his eyes upward to look into the intertwined canopy of heavily weighted branches and thickly woven vines, he noticed he had an audience. Four small white-faced monkeys were watching him in amusement. Their heads tilted this way and that as if they wondered what manner of entertainment they were about to enjoy.

Jim let out his breath slowly, relaxed his shoulders, and smiled weakly. Then he sunk back against the tree trunk and closed his eyes for a moment. His mind began to pick up speed.

At once he was painfully aware of how alone he was among the other species in the forest. There seemed to be no other humans in existence. Then his mind flashed a scene from an old "Twilight Zone" episode where a submarine commander was the only survivor of a nuclear war. The captain had walked through town after town searching for another person.

Ten thousand terrors paraded their awful outcomes before him. What had become of the others in his safari group. Had they even survived the poacher attack? Where were the scouts from the Safari Adventure Company? Was anyone even looking for him?

The crackling of a large, rotted branch breaking off and landing with a thud nearby brought Jim back to reality. He must concentrate on finding a way back to the compound. Jumping to his feet, he secured his backpack, got a firm grip on Weinberg's machete, and began clearing his way toward the east and the hill they had seen the day before.

He had been hard at work for probably thirty minutes and he felt he was making good headway. He could see that the forest looked lighter ahead and picked up his pace in hope. Maybe it was a road or at least a clearing. His ears were straining to hear any sound of rescue or predator as he chopped and tried to ignore the continual noise from the forest.

As he parted two large palm leaves, Jim was nearly blinded by the bright sunlight. A road! He had found a road! He stumbled happily onto the red dusty tire tracks and closed his eyes thankfully.

Ah, Benjamin would be so proud of him now! He'd made it through the training, he'd come to Africa, been pushed to the limit, and he had found the main road again!

Benjamin. He seemed light years away. Jim's preconceived idea of the safari was so idyllic compared to the ordeal he'd gone through. He suddenly became aware of the moment and the incredible power of his own personal adventure. "Everyone has his own adventure," the Dutchman had said, talking about green peas. "Each person will see this thing through his or her own unique eyes."

Jim definitely had his own story to tell. He had to make it back! He would survive and live to tell! In that moment the desire to tell the others of Weinberg's bravery, and Jim's passion to live, became the missing diamond. He began to live on purpose.

As he looked up toward the sun he tried to get a bearing of his location. Tenderly touching the caked blood on his shirt from the chest wound, he began walking east. After a half mile, Jim saw something up ahead on the road. Forgetting any danger, he sprinted toward it.

He stopped suddenly with surprise. It was the remains from the group's camp that he and Weinberg had found before. Not much was left behind by the poachers. Remembering where he had found Gabriel's body, Jim avoided looking that direction.

Well, at least this meant he knew where he was. Maybe he could find some more supplies. He began rummaging through the demolished tents.

After being hidden by the dense jungle for so many hours, Jim felt very exposed in the openness of the campsite. Looking up and over his shoulder he wondered if anyone was watching him. He wasn't sure which he was more frightened of—the possibility of another panther or the poachers. Realizing the dangers again, he scrambled to his feet and darted for the forest's camouflage at the side of the road, his arms full of new-found supplies.

Sitting in the bush he ate thankfully from the tins and packets he had salvaged from the dismal campsite. He decided to head back up the road to the west. They had only driven for a day from the Lodge at the Lake of Stars. Surely there had been some type of search started after the loss of radio contact with the group. Besides, it was mostly downhill and would be more familiar than the unknown route farther along to the halfway station.

Jim cleaned and dressed the wound on his chest as best he could. The blood had made it look a lot worse than it actually was. He bandaged it and changed into a clean shirt from one of the bags at the campsite.

Feeling more confident, he carefully packed up the things he decided to take. At least he still had his special hat! What a memento it would be in the years to come!

He walked out of the jungle and headed west, back toward the Lake of Stars. Past the burned out Jeep he stopped at the top of the ridge to look back at the valley. How beautiful it had seemed as he and Weinberg pulled up that first sunset afternoon. He remembered how Weinberg had grabbed the wheel to keep them from hitting the Jeep ahead. He smiled sadly, then turned to walk down the hill to the west.

After walking only a few paces, there came a sound like a Jeep engine off in the distance. Jim could not tell which direction in which it was coming. From the west, yes! It was coming from the west! It must be some sort of rescue team from the lodge. Jim stood in the middle of the road and waited. Soon the Jeep was in sight. As it drew closer Jim began to wave his arms. The figures in the Jeep pointed toward him and the sound of the engine said the vehicle was speeding up.

The Jeep slipped out of sight around a bend at the bottom of the hill and reappeared, now much closer. Jim could see the logo of the Safari Adventure Company on the front of the Jeep, but something was wrong. Big wrong. The faces of the men in the Jeep were suddenly clearer. There was an armed man standing in the back. It was the poachers!

Jim froze in terror as the man in the back raised the high powered rifle to his face and fired! The Jeep lurched as it grazed a rock and the shot spattered the red dirt a few yards behind him. Terrified, he ran back past the burnt out Jeep and into the jungle until he found himself on the trail that led back to the Mission.

"Oh no!" he panicked. "This is the road they came down after killing the guide!"

Jim pushed off the path and deeper into the trees. The poachers stopped the Jeep at the edge of the jungle and all the men jumped to the ground and followed. They shouted instructions in some unknown African dialect and fired their weapons in the direction they had last seen Jim.

Running for his life, he felt like a frightened hunted animal. The poachers were having great sport. They were expert hunters and much better at making their way through the jungle. Jim was terrible at both and worse at being an elusive prey.

Every time he thought he was safe he would pause to let his heart stop pounding only to hear the sound of the men approaching again.

"They are tracking me!" he thought and another wave of helpless terror swept over him.

It seemed like hours when he finally came to a fast moving narrow stream. He jumped down into the water and made a snap decision to go to the left. If he was right this would take him back and eventually lead him to the road heading east to the halfway station. He would follow the stream for a while to hide his trail from the trackers and then change direction. Maybe the water would throw them off like it did hound dogs in the movies!

Leaving the water about a half-mile down, he pushed ahead toward the west. Finally he stopped and sat down with his back against a tree and tried to collect himself. He closed his eyes as his breath came down to normal.

So tired....

So sleepy....

Just a little rest....

He closed his eyes and drifted off.

The sharp crack of a snapping twig woke him suddenly. He opened his eyes to another world. It was almost dark. He scrambled to his feet. Peering into the bush he strained in the bluish gray of the dusk to see if poacher, panther or any other danger were nearby. Jim eased the pistol out and released the safety. His throat was too tight to swallow. He had no desire at all to shoot anyone, but in the dim twilight, half-mad with fear, he was ready to deal with any situation with lethal force.

As his eyes adjusted to the shadows, he saw him! The lone poacher was about 30 yards away crouching in the bush. He was wearing army camouflage fatigues and raising his rifle slowly to his eye. In the split second that changes so many lives Jim pointed the pistol and fired three times directly toward the poacher. Out of the corner of his eye he saw the man roll to his side, whether from being shot, or to take cover, Jim did not wait to find out.

Still holding the pistol, Jim ducked down and grabbed his pack, then carefully backed around the tree and sprinted off in the direction he had been heading. He ran a few steps toward through the trees when all at once he was staring into an endless valley and teetering on the edge of a gigantic cliff! He had already lost his balance and could could not stop. Jim felt his stomach lurch into his throat as he fell over the edge!

He thrashed his arms wildly to find something to grab but there was nothing but air. It was too fast to scream. He fell for what seemed like an eternity then felt himself crashing into the branches of a tree and slamming down to the ground with a thud. Now rolling and sliding at incredible speed down the hill.

The last thing he remembered was his head slamming into something solid, sending him into blackness as he continued to deadfall, straight down the mountain.

Monkey in the Water

The tall grass swayed gracefully in the gentle breeze of another morning on the golden Savannah. The first beams of dawn awoke the local neighborhood and the sound of life was up again and about its business. The sky was deep blue and clear except for a lone vulture that had begun to circle hopefully. Its potential breakfast was lying face down at the bottom of the steep hill that emptied out on to the wide grassy plain.

Jim was awakened by the soreness of his shoulder and ribs. He rolled over on his back. Staring straight up into the sky, the madness of his situation came back to him one more time. He looked up at the mountain and saw the bluff from where he must have fallen. It made him sick to see that he had fallen over one hundred feet before hitting the ground! He had luckily crashed through the branches of some trees that cushioned his fall. Otherwise he would surely have died.

He thought of the man he had fired his pistol on the night before. Was he dead, wounded, or worse, still looking for him? The poachers must have given up and assumed Jim could not have survived the fall, that is if they even came this far. Jim was beyond caring about the poachers, though.

This was worse than any nightmare, but there was no use in running, he thought. Instead of jumping up and trying to frantically take some foolish action, Jim just lay there and thought. I am absolutely lost. I am tired, weak and hurt. He put his hand on an enormous painful lump on the top of his head and then on his aching shoulder. He arched his back to relieve his ribs and the sting of the panther cuts reported their presence.

"I am so hungry! My backpack must be gone. I could actually starve out here!" His fears ran wild, creating endless scenes of destruction. Just then he sensed the shadow of the vulture pass overhead and realized he was looking at him! "Oh, great! I have already been assigned to natures garbage machine."

Lying there wrapped in an endless wave of self-pity and fear, something new happened to Jim. Something he thought he had forgotten how to do. He began to cry. It welled up from deep within his soul. At first the slow coughing, then a moaning sob, and then he turned back over on his face and let go. He cried like a baby. Drawing handfuls of grass into his blood streaked, white-knuckled fists, he writhed and wailed, beyond comfort.

What a fool to come to Africa at a time like this in his life! What foolish choices had led him to lose his job. Why in the world had he made so many mistakes in his life? He wept and thought of them all. Every single one. He longed to hold his wife, his daughter, his son.

"I have been a total failure as a husband, as a father, oh dear God, as a man!" He wanted to just give up but there was no one to accept his surrender. That just made it worse.

His salty tears stung the scratches on his face. He rubbed them into his eyes with his fist. Bitterly, he cursed God, nature, his life, and the stinking, sorry Safari Adventure Company. He wanted to die.

Turning on his side again, he glimpsed something in the grass. A jackal hesitated a moment then darted away. He had been drawn by the sound of his crying. Jim got to his knees, then got to his feet, and stood in the waist high grass.

He traced his fall down the hillside and found his backpack. A little farther ahead he was excited to see his hat.

"Hello, old friend," he said sadly, as he slapped it against his thigh to remove the caked dirt. It was good to see anything familiar.

Gently tucking it back on his head he looked around at the wide plain. Somewhere he could hear the sound of water. Realizing how very thirsty he was he moved in the direction of the sound. The grass sloped down to a beautiful river, moving along at an easy pace. It was crystal clear and inviting. Jim knelt down and cupped his hands to drink. He noticed an inviting sandbar a few yards upstream and headed for it.

Easing his backpack to the ground he undressed and slipped into the cold water. It had the effect of numbing his scratches and insect bites, giving him a little relief. He rolled over on his back and floated. There was a wild mango tree on the other shore. He pulled two ripe mangoes down and ate them, savoring each sweet bite. The training films he had seen at camp came back to him as well as the words of the trainer.

"To some the jungle is a terror, full of evil and threat, ready to kill anyone who happens to venture in," Nina had said at the banquet, quoting her father. "To others, who are wise and know its ways, the jungle is a veritable paradise. It is full of food and medicine and materials for shelter and all kinds of tools. Learn of these, and you could live in the jungle forever and never want for anything."

Jim stayed in the river for a long time. The mangoes were excellent for breakfast so he had one more for dessert. As he sat in the shallow water near the sandbar the water flowed across his chest as just his head stuck out of the water. He thought of a picture in *National Geographic* he had seen as a boy. There was some kind of northern monkey neck deep in frigid water. His fur was spiked with ice and his red face was contorted in a fierce grimace, intended to frighten the photographer.

Jim laughed, remembering the picture in his mind and then began to try to mimic the monkey faces. When he realized what he was doing he laughed louder, "Ouch!" He felt the sting of the cut on his ribs and put his hand to his side.

How, he wondered, could he be wailing and suicidal one moment and then laughing the next? Perhaps dementia was setting in. Maybe he was cracking up under the strain. If he was going insane he sure didn't feel like. In fact he felt in control! There was something fundamentally different about Jim, but he couldn't put his finger on it. Maybe, at the loss of everything, he was left with all he really ever controlled — his choices.

The morning sun was warming up and Jim lay on the sand until he was dry. He snoozed a little, while watching for the vulture. The sandbar wound around the bend of the river and backed up against some large trees. Jim walked to the trees and hung the clothes he had rinsed in the river out to dry.

He explored the contents of his backpack. Finding some medicine, he treated the bigger cuts and scrapes on his body. He noted a couple of packs of crackers and granola bars. *The Three Treasures* fell out onto the sand, face down. Jim picked up the book and saw there was writing inside the cover.

"To Jim with best regards. May you come to understand that the most important treasures are the ones that have nothing at all to do with our external circumstances. Your companion and friend. Weinberg."

"He sneaked in there and wrote this," said Jim, tears welling in his eyes.

He thumbed through the pages thoughtfully. The power of Weinberg's selfless sacrifice was impossible to rationalize in worldly terms. He could have saved himself. Instead he chose, voluntarily, to give his life for his friend.

He paused at the "Treasure of the Heart" and silently read the words again. They seemed to come to life in his hands as it became clear what was meant by the power of loving and sacrificially giving to others. Jim recalled the words of Weinberg as he thought about the monks at the monastery.

"What incredibly valuable lives," he had said.

That was the exact legacy he would assign to Weinberg. Jim now realized his sadness was for himself, not for Weinberg. Jim was alone and missed his friend but he knew with a wonderful certainty that the older man was keeping the appointment he said he had with his wife. Knowing this gave him an overpowering sense of well-being.

Reaching the end of "The Treasure of the Heart" he came to the third treasure. Turning the page he saw the title, "The Treasure of the Spirit." Jim had never read this last part of the book. He was too turned off by religion so he had not wanted to hear about this "spirit-stuff."

With his wet clothes drying and the mood created by finding Weinberg's autograph, Jim sat in the sand next to the river and read on. He surely owed the man that much.

The Third Treasure

THE TREASURE OF THE SPIRIT

If you have begun to gather treasures of the heart, you have started to realize the incredible power in the discipline of self-denial and seeking the welfare of others. Of those who embark on this journey, many travelers stop at the Treasure of the Heart. Some have become great humanitarians, making valuable contributions to society. Others have simply lived this principal out in their corners of the world, becoming pillars of communities or just very well liked friends.

If you should stop and not pursue this last treasure, you will be making the most tragic of errors! There will come a point in your life when you will find solace nowhere in the first two. You will ache inside in a way only those who have felt this pain can know.

We have discovered that even after fame, friends, money, and all manor of accomplishment, one must stand before the mirror and answer two questions. One, how do I find absolution in this life for the things I have done for which I am ashamed. Two, what is to become of me at my death. There is one answer to both questions.

The answer lies in the truth. Of late, truth has been diluted by those that say that all truth is relative. That is absurd. If I were to take your watch and claim that "my truth" says you are to release it to me, in fact, my truth tells me you will be better off for learning this particular giving lesson, you would cry "foul!"

You would see instantly that there is a larger body of truth that governs our world. We all know it is wrong to steal, but how? The laws against stealing, though man made, are inspired by a higher law that we all know. Witness the fact that even when the law does not catch us doing wrong we feel guilty...to whom?

Guilty to the truth. Wrong in the ever presence of right. Where do we go to get square with the first question and the answer to the second? We believe you must go to ancient scripture. When Pontius Pilate stood and asked the carpenter from Nazareth "what is truth?" he was unknowingly making a statement to the world about the silent prisoner and the pride of man. Truth was standing in front of him, but he refused to see.

The carpenter told his followers he was sent from God. He said "I am the way, the truth, and the life, no man cometh to the Father but by me." If you or I were to make this claim we would have some serious challenges on our hands. A decision must be made. There are three options. One, either he was insane and deluded, which hardly squares with the incredible clarity of his life and words. Two, he was a liar who knew he was lying and was willing to die for this absurd fantasy, or, three, he really was who he claimed to be.

Upon examination of his life and words the first two options seem unlikely. If the third is true then it is imperative that he be sought. In the treasure of the heart we are given the road that leads to joy. In the treasure of the spirit we are called by the Master to walk this road and respond to his simple words, "follow me."

Beware the false roads and false leaders! They are persuasive and attractive because they appeal to human pride and reason. There is but one truth and one way that leads to life! It sounds huge and impossible, to travel with this power. Pilate's drama reveals to us that truth is not a concept, Truth is a person. The miracle is that the moment you begin to seek him with all your heart, on His terms, not lugging along your preconceived illusions, the finding is already thus assured.

"You will seek me and find me when you search for me with your whole heart."

—Jeremiah 29:13

Jim replaced the small book in his pack and sat very, very still. He looked across the river at a tree that had been invaded by beautiful yellow and blue birds. They were singing a sweet and primitive song and hopping from branch to branch. The awesomeness of nature seemed to speak to Jim and assure him that the song was for him alone. "The author of nature has dedicated a song to me," he said. He smiled and gathered his clothes from the tree and dressed.

Buoyed by the morning respite, Jim decided to follow the river. He looked upstream and downstream. Logic said the river would empty into the sea somewhere so Jim chose downstream. Perhaps because it looked like the upstream path might take him back toward the panther.

He hiked the route for the rest of the day, collecting fruits and other edibles on the way. His jungle training began to come back to him in this clearer frame of mind and his confidence returned with each small victory. Confidence aside, however, as darkness drew down on him, he was painfully aware that he was still completely lost.

Like a traveler who starts to evaluate the motels and restaurants he passes, he began looking out for a good place to camp for the night. Worry returned and nagged him. What if the river drew dangerous beasts, nocturnal hunters, toward him if he camped next to the stream? He would need to build a fire. Would the fire draw the poachers? Maybe it would draw a rescue? He decided to take the risk.

Finding a safe looking place where he could get his back to a stone outcropping, Jim lowered his pack to mark the spot and began to gather wood in the area. He spied a dead tree leaning across the bend in the river ahead and headed there. As he reached the tree he heard a distant crashing sound. He cautiously moved down the river to the ever-increasing volume of the noise. The river had widened and deepened as he had followed it that day but now it was moving much faster. Then he found the source of the sound.

Under the Nickel Moon

A waterfall! Jim smiled, thinking of all the cartoons where the unwitting character accidentally goes over the edge. He stepped out of the water sheepishly as if some force might sweep him over the top, and moved up along the bank to the overlook. What a magnificent view!

The waterfall was very high and hard to look at from the top. He gazed across the canyon and thought how much it looked like the place where he and Weinberg had sat and talked. Then he spied the stone bench across the gorge and the road that led back to the monastery.

Wait a minute. It was the exact same valley! Only now he was on the opposite side! He let out a yell and waved his hat over his head. He knew where he was! The joy of discovery mixed with the sadness he felt for losing his companion rushed together as he looked out on the special place.

Recalling the Jeep they had seen from the stone benches, he looked down the ridge to his right and sure enough way down there was the little dirt road used by the Safari Adventure Company! He recalled seeing a walking path along this side of the valley that would lead down to the road. He could be on the road in about two hours!

Looking back up the river where he had left his pack he knew it would be dark before he could descend the steep path. It would be extremely dangerous to try to navigate the trail at night. He would not risk disaster this close to victory. He would camp here at this lovely spot and make it down at sunrise. Perhaps someone would see his fire and send rescue in the morning.

Jim found lots of wood nearby and soon had a fine fire. He managed to boil some water in a small cup and added the leaves he had found to make an aromatic Wild African Tea. Munching on his harvest of the day, he waited for the tea to cool. He leaned back on the log near the fire and looked out at the beautiful valley. What had Weinberg said about it?

Oh, yes, he had said there were some places on earth where you could see the hand of God more clearly than others. Well, this was definitely one of them. There was more than the natural beauty of the place. There was a spiritual presence in the value of the brief time he had spent here with dear Weinberg. There was the hope he felt for finding the road that would lead him to safety. But, there was more.

Jim reached for the still hot tea and took a sip. "Wow that's hot!" he shouted to no one. But the feeling was as good as the pungent taste so he smacked his lips and went right back for another. Setting the cup on the rock next to him like a little coffee table, he tried to gather in his feelings.

He thought of something Weinberg had said at breakfast the second day of the safari. He had it his journal although it didn't seem to mean much then.

"Sometimes the most significant moments of our lives go right by unnoticed," he had said, "because we are too busy heading somewhere totally trivial. Usually the most valuable moments in life are only seen in hindsight. They are sweet enough when we look back on them but how much richer life is when we are actually there, in the moment. We must learn to taste, feel, and sense them as they happen. This way we heighten the experience, extend the moment and capture it in a richer, deeper way, that will last forever."

Jim closed the journal and remembered Weinberg's explanation.

"The words of a child," he had said, "the touch of a loved one, the unexpected opportunity and privilege to view the intensely vivid reality of life displayed by nature and chance. Feel your feet on the floor, your hand on the table, and the wind as it touches your face. Hear the sounds, and smell the smells. You can magnify the richness of the life you are already experiencing if you will commit, whenever you think of it, to consciously be where ever you are."

Jim let his eyes shift their focus and tried to amplify all his senses. A feeling of peace and contentment washed over him and bathed him in it's power. He opened his eyes and knew what it was that he was feeling. The power of this place was only partially the answer.

He was somehow different now that he had faced ultimate fear and survived. He felt the muscles in his arms and legs and knew he had been given the gift of a healthy body. He thought of all he had learned and would continue to learn with his new commitment to read books and listen to tapes when he returned home. His mind would become the engine that would transform his life.

His heart had melted at the story Weinberg had told about his marriage. He was already planning how to mend fences with Tracey and the kids. He had been the beneficiary of the greatest gift at the dearest price when Weinberg had saved his life. Never again would he be the same. He would do his best to become a giving, caring person and try to be worthy of the sacrifice this great man had made for him.

But the real difference was somewhere deep inside Jim's soul. "If anyone had told me I would be sitting alone, cut, scraped, and out of supplies at nightfall, lost in the jungle of Africa and been happy, I would have told them they were crazy." he thought. But it was true. He was strangely happy and content.

Reaching into his pack for the medicinal ointment, his hand discovered Weinberg's Bible. He pulled it out and looked at the cover. It was worn and soft from many hours of use. Benjamin had kidded him about its ragged condition back at the lodge and offered to buy him a new one.

"A Bible that is falling apart usually belongs to someone who isn't!" Weinberg had replied with his wink and thumbs-up and smile.

It occurred to him that he was holding a most precious keepsake that had become his to watch over now. Opening it carefully, reverently, he saw that there were lots of handwritten notes in the margins and hi-lighted verses in various markers and ink colors. It never occurred to him that anyone would write in a Bible. There were dates and names of speakers and little drawings and arrows indicating devotion and careful study.

The thin delicate pages crackled and turned easily to his careful touch. The book seemed so ancient and intense here beside the waterfall in the vast wilderness.

Jim turned to the table of contents and found the Gospel according to John. Benjamin had said that was a good place to start so he turned there and read the first three tiny chapters. He was instantly challenged by the words, "He came unto His own, and they knew Him not."

How strange, that the people, who had expected their Messiah for years, rejected him when he actually came. Jim thought about how that was kind of true in his own life. How many times had the simple message of salvation come to him while he ignored and scoffed at it?

Suddenly he felt like thanking God but he didn't know how. He thought about his father and mother. They had taken him to church off and on but it didn't seem to mean much to them. They never talked about spiritual things and Jim had never seen them pray anywhere outside of church. Jim, too, hadn't prayed since grade school and then only under the watchful eye of a Sunday School teacher.

He felt silly, but began with, "Now I lay me down to sleep..." and then stopped.

"If you seek me with all your heart you will find me," the third treasure had promised. If the heart meant the selfless giving to others that was totally outside of yourself, then seeking with the heart must mean you stop focusing on you, and search for God outside of yourself, on His terms.

Jim began again. This time he prayed a very humble prayer of thanks for all the things he had been given in his life. The more he listed, the more powerful and heartfelt were his words. He began to realize just how fortunate he was. He asked to be able to return home to his family and to make amends there. He asked for strength to follow the ideas in *The Three Treasures*.

Then he became silent. With his eyes closed he said, "These guys say, that you said, that if I will look for you with all of my heart, I will find you. Well, I am going to find out if that is true because I am going to try it. The first thing I'm going to do when I get back is to read this Bible they say you wrote and look that up, and see if it's there. Then, if it is, I'm going to read the whole thing. The rest is up to you. Thanks again. Amen."

When he opened his eyes he had that instant funny feeling you get when you enter a movie theater in the daylight and find it dark when you come out. Though he had only prayed a short time the sun had dipped below the trees behind him. Crickets began making sounds like the rusty hinge on an old screen door in the cooler air. The jungle prepared for another night.

Pulling the small tin cup to his lips he cautiously sampled the tea. It was just right. The sun was burning a laser show on the rock face below the stone bench across the canyon. The whole scene was breathtaking. No photograph in the world could capture its exhilarating color and texture. Every time he looked at a different area it seemed to change with the sinking sun and made for an almost liquid clarity.

The sky melted from pink to orange, to red, and then into darkness. The sun was replaced by a quarter moon that lit the valley in an eerie luminescent stillness. When his daughter, Claire, was little, he remembered they had been driving home, just the two of them. She was probably five or six. She had looked up and seen this shape of moon and proudly announced,

"Look, Daddy! A *nickel moon!*"

How he had treasured that innocence and joy. He had patiently explained what a quarter moon was. She had laughed with him and the nickel moon became their private little joke. They had even made up a little song about it. He sang it softly.

" I can almost see,
  A place where we can go together,
  You and Mom and me.
  Take short pants you'll love the weather
  Bears that care, and ponies fly,
  We can go right now.

Daddy, why do people work?
Always seem in such a hurry,
Don't they play no more?
Tired faces lined in worry
Sit down here with me,
Teddy's having tea.

Under the nickel moon,
Live on soda pop and candy,
Under the nickel moon,
Right next door to Ann and Andy
Bears that care, and ponies fly,
We can go right now.

Daddy why you look so sad?
Don't you think that we can go there?
Growing up's not bad
A part of us should always stay where,
We can always be,
Young and wild and free!
Under the nickel moon,
Live on soda pop and candy,
Under the nickel moon,
Right next door to Ann and Andy
Bears that care, and ponies fly,
We can go right now."

His voice broke at the last line. His throat would not let him go on singing. He bowed his head and sat quietly for a long time, then he started to write in his tattered journal. A flood of thoughts and impressions came too quickly for his pen. He tried to recall all Weinberg's words and wrote down what he could.

Before he stopped to sleep he wrote a long love-letter to Tracey. Feeling like a World War I doughboy writing from a foxhole in Europe, he romantically said all the things he wished he had told her when he had the chance. He described her beauty, their special names for one another, and how he treasured the secret moments only the two of them could ever know.

He savored the preciousness of the hard times when they were young, trying to work and raise the babies. He boldly poured out his heart to his wife in case the journal was found, and he had not made it out alive. His heart was filled with such powerful love and emotion. He could not help but cry again.

This time tears of joy and hope and love replaced the bitter sorrow he had tasted only this morning. He wiped his eyes with the soft hand-kerchief from his pocket, sat back and took a deep breath. He replaced the journal in his pack and made it his pillow. Fiddling with the fire for a bit, he drank the last of the tea and never knew it when sleep came.

Dangerous Rescue

Jim wasted no time in putting out the smoldering fire and starting down the trail to the road. The sun, now rising on the opposite side of the valley, lit and warmed the face of the wall he was descending. "I wish I had some sunglasses," he thought, then another thought replaced it that made him smile. "But, I am sure glad I have eyes!" His new attitude was energizing. He looked for ways to replace the negative thoughts he normally had with new, powerful, positive ones.

Sure enough the path led down to the road. He could glimpse the road every time the path wound to the outside of the ledge. It was a trail, but it was pretty rough going. He would have been crazy to try to take this path in the dark last night. He calculated that he would be down to the road in about a half-hour. Then it would be only a matter of time until he either came to the half-way station or a friendly Jeep came along. He felt strong and confident that the end of this journey was near.

Suddenly the air was pierced by a shriek. Where had he heard the sound before? Loud and begging, it was the wail of a woman screaming for her life. The sound echoed across the canyon. Jim stopped and tried to pinpoint its origin.

Gunshots rang out, then a crazy whoop, followed by a wicked laughter. There in the valley, on the other side of the river, were two people running. One of them was Karin!

She was being chased by one of the poachers. It was not the same one he had shot at before falling down the cliff. The long-haired filthy bandit was short and stout and gaining fast on the ragged girl. Her clothes were tattered and torn. The poacher stopped briefly and fired his gun around her and laughed sadistically. It was obvious as she stumbled and fell that she was exhausted and terrorized. The torture continued.

She was trying to run up the path on the side of the valley where Jim and Weinberg had sat so idyllic just a few days and a thousand years ago. She was near the top, but the path there was steep and she slipped and slid down right into the hands of the poacher.

Jim crouched, frozen in the bushes, too far away to do anything else, he watched the man brutally punch her face and knock her unconscious. He then pulled a piece of cord from his pack and tied her hands together tightly. That was when Jim saw the other two men standing right where he and Weinberg had sat by the flowers. What absolute horror she must have been in as she tried to escape the trap.

The larger man picked her up and slung her over his shoulder easily. The trio disappeared back up the path toward the monastery.

A thousand excuses went through Jim's mind. How could he expect to do anything about Karin? He was weak and exhausted himself. His hand traced the wound from the panther's claws. Then a new thought came to his mind—a thought of pure courage. He could not go on to safety knowing the girl was in the hands of these savage men. He would do the right thing. He would give everything he had to save her! The minute he made the decision the knots in his stomach tightened and threatened to make him ill but he fought his own fear with confident action.

He descended the rest of the path quickly and paddled hard across the rapidly moving river with the help of a log to keep his pack dry and reached the top of the cliff in an hour. Stopping briefly to catch his breath at the stone bench he surveyed the waterfall one more time. He had been certain he would never see the waterfall again and the power of the place swept over him once more. He instantly flashed on the vision of Weinberg sitting next to him and saying, "There are some places where you can see the hand of God," he had said, "this is mine."

Jim realized that another place you could see God's hand at work was in the life of a person who had voluntarily chosen to give themselves to someone else, regardless of the cost. Weinberg had painted this beautiful picture with his rescue of Jim from the panther. He would not waste the gift!

"I know I was not worth the price Weinberg paid," thought Jim, "but, he didn't save me because of who I was, but because of the great treasure of sacrificial giving to the one in need. He didn't even think twice. The decision was made long ago."

The thought was like a lightning bolt of strength. He leapt up from the stone bench and committed himself down the path toward the monastery. He would not turn back!

The sun was already high and hot through the trees when he peered over the last hill and saw the monastery. His shirt clung to his skin drenched with perspiration. Jim had no plan. He was just going to show up and do what he could. There was no sign of the poachers or

Karin, so he made his way into the bushes where he and Weinberg had spent that awful night. He couldn't help but look at the ashes of the bonfire, but, thankfully, there was nothing left of the body to see.

He pulled the pistol out and released the safety. Jim didn't even own a gun. He hadn't hunted since ten years ago with his father, but the grip felt good in his hand. He would shoot the poachers, if he had to! That's all there was to it. There might be only the three of them left since they had killed one of their own and he might have shot the other. Jim realized he was hoping that he had killed the man in the forest. He was operating completely out of survival instinct now.

Rounding the corner of the monastery he saw the secret passage where he and Weinberg had escaped. He started to squeeze in when a jolt of intense fear iced him where he stood.

"Dear God," he thought, "what if they catch me and kill me?"

"But what if this were Tracey, or Claire?"

"What if they were in great danger and needed a rescuer. Wouldn't I pray that a stranger would take action?"

"Of course!"

"But, why me?"

"Oh, God! Why me?"

Right in the middle of his old nature screaming out in fear and selfishness, Jim knew the awful reality of the situation. Just then a divine guidance, beyond his own understanding or experience, filled him with the courage and strength, not to run, but to face his terror and act.

He understood clearly that in the entire world of people, he was the one and only person on the planet who could do anything to help this poor doomed girl. The old Jim, weak and afraid, died right there on the spot. He prayed for strength and safety, swallowed hard, and slipped into the small opening in the side of the stone monastery, and into the darkness of the rooms.

He was plunged into the blackness of the monk's cell. The damp coolness of the place jumped on his sweaty shirt and skin. He waited for his eyes to adjust to the darkness then flipped on Weinberg's flashlight and crept cautiously down the hallway like a cat burglar. Gun drawn and pointed he shoved his canvas pack back up on his shoulder and began to look into each room.

No sight or sound of either Karin or the poachers. He looked over the last room and turned his head toward the chapel. The colored stones were bathing the chapel in a rainbow of blue, red, amber and green. The gun boxes had been opened and several of the rifles had been scattered across the pews in the front. Most of the tusks were gone. The poachers had been very busy.

Turning back down the hall, Jim strained to hear anything at all. Silence. There was still one room past the passageway he had not checked. He slipped softly down the hall and shined the light into the small cell. The words "I can do all things through Christ, who strengthens me," were right in the center of his light. Jim's mouthed the words silently as he read them.

Forcing his eyes to look into the dim shadows he saw Karin huddled against the wall in a fetal position, silent and still.

"Please, please, don't let her be dead," he thought.

He moved quickly to her side and touched her face. It was streaked with blood, dirt, and tears. Whether from the poachers or her days in the jungle, he could not tell. He marveled at her courage. How in the world did she survive?

Her bound hands shot up to her face as she opened her eyes, seeing only the flashlight.

She flinched and whimpered, "Please don't hurt me anymore," covering her face. The red marks on her wrists revealed how hard she tried to be free.

"Karin," he whispered, "its me, Jim." He pulled the flashlight out of her face and pointed it up, bathing the room in a soft yellow dimness.

"Oh, God!" she said half choking, "I can't believe it. How in the world did you get here?"

Her feisty spirit had been practically extinguished as her hope had faded. After being lost for days in the jungle and captured by the poachers she had started to believe she was going to die at the end of unthinkable captivity.

Lifting his finger to his lips he gave her a sign for silence.

"Where are the poachers?" he whispered quickly, cutting the rope from her hands with his pocketknife.

"I heard them talking after they threw me in here. Two of them were going to the village to get whiskey. I don't know where the other one is," she said, frantically untangling the ropes and reaching for the cord around her ankles.

"Are there three or four?" he asked.

"Just three."

"Okay, let's get out of here. There's a secret passageway to the outside. We just have to go back into the hall and into the next room. Follow me."

With that Jim helped her to her feet. She was bruised badly but the determination that made her so tough became her friend. Jim took her arm and led her to the door.

"Okay, let's go." said Jim. It looked like a perfect escape from the monastery when he heard the shout.

"Aiyee-ahhhh!" came the warlike scream from the guarding poacher. Jim shined the flashlight toward the sound. He came from the direction of the front courtyard and was heading straight for them. The flashlight reflected back a laser glint off the biggest machete Jim had ever seen in his life.

Jim pushed Karin behind him down the hall. She ran. With no way of knowing, she shot past the room with the escape door, and headed toward the chapel at the end of the hallway where the guns were stored. Now they were trapped!

Jim spun around and pulled his pistol to fire but the machete caught his arm with a glancing blow and knocked the gun from his hand. As it clattered on the stone floor, blood spurted from the gash. Jim cried out and put his other hand on the wound as an instant reaction.

The poacher laughed. Jim knew right away that this was the sadistic torturer who had fired at Karin as he chased her. The one who had punched the helpless girl! He looked at the stubble-bearded face and the yellow stained teeth and realized that all his misfortune, the death of Weinberg, Karin and his burning arm, were all the fault of the evil man in front of him.

Instead of running, Jim doubled his fist and smashed old yellow teeth right in the mouth. Blood drained out of the startled poacher's mouth. Fire shot up Jim's arm from the blow as his fist was cut on the foul teeth. Before the attacker could recover from the punch, Jim kicked him solidly in the groin.

Remarkably, the poacher caught Jim's leg and threw him quickly on his back. Jim scrambled to feel for the pistol but it was gone. He rolled on his side just as the clang of the machete sent sparks from the stone floor in the dim hallway by his head.

He half crawled, half ran, scrambling furiously toward the chapel. The poacher was right on his heels. Out of the corner of his eye he saw Karin pressed flat against the wall just inside the doorway. As the bandit reached the entrance she swung the rifle by the barrel, like a baseball bat, with all her might and smashed the stock of the heavy gun into the poacher's face. The impact of the strike, combined with his running momentum knocked the poacher off his feet and flat on his back.

Jim watched in shock as she took her redemption. In one motion she spun the gun around in her hand and fired every round into the lurching body until both the gun and the devilish fiend were silent. Jim thought of the panther and understood. In one horrible moment she destroyed the destroyer. Jim never knew what happened to her at the hands of the men, and he never asked.

There in the stained glass light of the chapel Karin stood, eyes wide, chest heaving, she panted. Staring down at her dead tormentor, she dropped the hot smoking gun and began to weep. She drew her clinched fists to her temples and moaned. It was the most heartbreaking sound Jim had ever heard.

Jim ran to her side and held her as the sulfur smell of gunpowder permeated the room. Finally, she calmed down enough to follow him out to the passage to freedom.

Knowing that the other two poachers had only been gone a short time, Jim led Karin back up the trail to the waterfall where they rested and tended to each other's wounds. Jim was badly cut from the machete but she fixed a good tight bandage that stopped the bleeding. He used the medicine he had in his bag to take the sting out of her many cuts. She was not as seriously hurt as he thought at first. She was, however, very dehydrated, and hadn't eaten much in the days since the attack.

She told Jim how the poachers had come upon them late that morning. They wore masks and intended to rob the safari. When the little man with the wicked laugh grabbed her at the campsite and started to drag her away, Rosa stepped in and slapped him. A fight broke out. Then gunshots. Everyone ran into the jungle in chaos. She never saw any of the group again. She had wandered in circles and was just about to give up when she was spotted by the poachers.

"You saved my life, Jim. I am so very, very thankful for you. Oh bless you. I will never forget what you did for me. You could have left me behind and not risked your life, but you did. Thank you, Jim, thank you, from the bottom of my heart."

As she hugged his neck, Jim knew in a new way what the Treasure of the Heart was all about. He was receiving something wonderful that only came from giving. The power of the moment would last forever!

Jim reminded her that she had saved his life, too! Her quick thinking in the chapel to find and load one of the rifles saved them both. He was very grateful. He told her the story of what happened to Weinberg as they headed back to the road down the path that had started it all.

She wondered aloud about Rosa. They were just beginning to build a friendship. Was she alive? What about the others?

They emerged from the jungle at the original campsite. Except for the burned out Jeep it was picked clean. The body of the guide was gone.

Jim told Karin how he had taken up some things from here as he doubled back. They agreed, though, that the poachers had probably returned and cleaned the site of all the supplies and equipment.

Then they saw the handmade sign.

"Please stay near the road. We are searching for you," it announced. At the bottom of the stick that held it was a backpack filled with food, medicine and supplies.

Close Call

They gathered up the wonderful care package, as they called it, ate a little and decided to get as far from the campsite as they could. Battered but determined, the new friends set out.

It grew late and long shadows crossed the road. They kept an eye out for a place to camp for the night. The weary adventurers were headed in the direction of the lake again. This time they descended alone. No poachers with rifles greeted them as they walked.

The going was easy here on the road but Jim stayed alert. He listened for the sound of danger. They agreed that if they heard a vehicle they would hide in the bushes and look to see if it were carrying poachers or not. He would rather walk all the way if necessary than take a chance of falling prey to them again. They would surely be out to kill after finding their dead companion at the monastery.

In the distance, they heard the sound of an engine. Leaping into the jungle they realized that they had just turned a corner and would not be able to identify the occupants until just as the Jeep was passing. If the driver was friendly, they would then have to jump out and try to flag them down in a split second, just as they passed. They crouched hopefully, ready to spring. Jim prayed silently for a friendly face.

The whine of the engine lowered and then started rising again as the driver down shifted to make the hill. Just as the Jeep came into sight Jim saw two of the men he recognized from the Safari Adventure Company looking straight ahead.

He sprang out of the bush just as they passed, nearly hitting the back of the Jeep with his hand. The men never saw him as he stood in the road behind them and danced and waved his hands, screaming at the top of his lungs.

"Don't leave us!" they cried. "Hey! Hey! Help! Help! Help!"

The blaring horn behind them made them both jump and spin around suddenly in shock.

A second Jeep!

It darted away and barely missed hitting Jim at full speed. He fell away on the side of the road and lay there with his heart pounding. All that he had been through to die in a car wreck a thousand miles from a traffic light!

"I was nearly killed, again!" he thought as he tried to stand.

"Jim! My God, Jim! Is that you?" called a familiar voice. The Jeep, which had stopped, was now backing up toward him. "Oh thank God, it is!"

Jim rolled over and sat up on his elbow just as Benjamin and Stephen bailed out of each side of the Jeep and ran to his side.

"How in the world did you come to be here?" cried Benjamin. "We have been lookin' all over for you!"

"It's a long story, Benjamin. Man is it good to see your face, and Jeep!" said Jim as the men helped him to his feet.

The others from the first Jeep were attending to Karin, who had no complaints, this time, about anything.

"Where is Weinberg?" Benjamin asked as he saw the blood and cuts all across Jim's battered body.

"He is dead, Benjamin," said Jim sadly. "He was killed by a panther. He took my place. He saved my life." Now that he was safe, the words stuck in his throat as the magnitude of the whole experience began to dawn on him.

"Come on, man, let's get you back to camp." He placed his arm around Jim's waist. Benjamin and Stephen loaded Jim carefully into the back seat and arranged their supplies so he could lie back comfortably.

Stephen filled in the rest of the story. He told Jim how the poachers had come upon them and held them up at gunpoint. They wore masks and would have gotten everything with no resistance from the group until one of them began to grab Karin. Rosa slapped him and was shoved to the ground. B.B. Chang, the younger Japanese man had kicked the tormentor in the face and everything broke loose into confusion. The group scattered in fear and ran into the jungle in different directions while B.B. and Gabriel fought with the poachers.

Gabriel was shot and killed and Ishido was wounded and left for dead. The poachers stole what they could. They took two of the Jeeps, one wouldn't start so they figured it was broken down. They set the other one on fire.

It was then that Jim saw the large bandage on Stephen's shoulder under his oversized shirt. He did not have to ask what had happened to him. Benjamin explained how Stephen, seriously wounded, had tried valiantly to gather the scattered band and bring them back to safety.

Jim realized he and Weinberg had arrived after the group had returned to camp. It was total coincidence that they had not run into each other before the storm.

Jim thought about the intensity of the storm that night as Stephen told how he'd been able to round up everyone but Karin. They drove the roads looking for signs of their companions until finally they gave up and left the area to get Ishido to a doctor.

Stephen had volunteered to return to the area to get his friend's body and to search for the three lost ones. He was very grateful to find Jim and Karin. Somehow it seemed to lighten the load of responsibility he felt as the emergency leader of the group.

The Safari Company put up such an uproar that the government authorities were forced to do something and were tracking down the poachers even now. Jim told the men about the monastery hide out.

"Now it is over," said Stephen as he guided the Jeep along the dusty road. Now that everyone has been found, things can get back to normal around here."

"Back to normal?" thought Jim. Things would never be back to normal again in his life. The steady drone of the engine, excitement and fatigue took their toll on Jim. He slumped back on the blankets and drifted into sleep as the driver guided the Jeep down the road toward the station.

Over and Out!

"Hey, wait a minute! Stop! I need to talk to that guy!" Despite the noise of the rotors Jim heard the voice behind him as he was stepping up onto the deck of the helicopter. He turned to see Andy running toward the aircraft, his huge smile unmistakable across the landing zone. Benjamin trailed him by a few steps.

"Hey, lightweight, you taking the sissy way home?" he kidded loudly. "I can't believe you are going to wimp out on me!"

"Yeah, Andy, I am going to leave Africa to the real hosses like you!" He smiled back warmly as Andy and he pumped each other's hands. "They said you had come back here and joined the search party for me. Thanks so much! Thank you both."

"Have you talked to your wife yet?" said Andy.

"Not yet. We played radio tag though," Jim said referring to the wireless set at the halfway station. "They told me she was frantic when she heard I was lost."

"Some guys will do anything to get attention," kidded Andy.

"Now I know why you had me sign a liability release," said Jim. "If you had charged me, I think I'd demand a refund."

"Jim, I am afraid we will have to charge you double. You were not supposed to have such an intense safari," Benjamin joked.

"Seriously, my friend, I am so sorry you had to go through what you have," Benjamin said patting Jim's good arm.

"Thanks, Benjamin. I'm okay. I am just trying to process everything. Thank you for taking the time for me back at the lake. Your words meant a lot. There's a bigger reason why I experienced what I did."

"I like you, Jim. You have come a long way. Give me a call in a couple of weeks, after you are up and around. I think I have an idea for a job you may be very interested in." Benjamin stepped along the landing gear to talk to Karin who was already in the passenger seat next to the pilot.

"Jim, I found what I was looking for all these years," said Andy seriously. "Except it wasn't in Africa at all, buddy, it was all around me. I am taking The Three Treasures very seriously when I get home." Andy pointed to his temple, then poked his chest, then pointed to the sky.

Jim nodded and smiled at Andy's meaningful pantomime and did the same. Pulling his finger down from the sky, he pointed at Andy and shouted, "You are the man!" then opened his hand to offer his handshake.

Still shaking hands, both men reached their free arm around the other and hugged tightly for an extra moment.

"Keep in touch, Jungle Jim."

"You do the same, Andy."

Stepping up on the deck of the helicopter Jim turned around and saw the light in the eyes of his friend. They each knew that they had both indeed found the path to the truth that had been missing all their lives. Andy and Benjamin hugged Karin. They stepped back and saluted her. She smiled broadly and waved back.

"So long, Andy," shouted Jim over the helicopter engines as they began to rev up. "I guess the adventure is over."

"No way, Jim!" shouted Andy over the clatter. "Don't you understand? *The greatest adventure is the rest of your life!*"

As the rotors increased in speed the wind whipped hard on the hair and clothes of Andy and Benjamin. A grinning Andy stepped up leaned into the force and gave Jim the crazy sideways thumbs up sign.

The helicopter lifted up slowly and banked to the East toward Lilongwe and the Kamuzu Airport. Jim watched as Andy waved until he disappeared under the sweeping forest. As he looked down on the place where he had spent the last few terrifying days he took a moment to reflect on the intense power of the human desire to live.

The beautiful waterfall appeared below as Jim shook his head in disbelief. Who would believe his amazing tale? Though he was down there only a few short hours ago, already it started to seem surreal and dreamlike.

He knew, however, that he was different. Right down the center of his being he would never, ever, be the same again.

As he settled back, his thoughts turned to Tracey and the kids. He knew what his destiny held. He would turn his mind to truth and wisdom. He would learn to be the best husband, father, and person, he could be. He had faith that the simple act of giving, repeated over time, would open his life like a fountain of meaning and power. It would not be easy to repair years of neglect. But, he would stay the course.

Finally he knew that he was already standing in the doorway of spiritual truth. He put his hand in his jacket and pulled out Weinberg's tattered Bible. Of all the insane events of the last two weeks, the fact that he now held this precious book from that incredible man, was unexplainable by any other means, but one.

There was a force far greater than anything Jim had ever known, that was drawing him into total clarity and reality. In the words of the Third Treasure, "The miracle is that the moment one begins to seek with all their heart, the finding is already thus assured!"

Jim tucked the Bible back into his jacket and closed his eyes. The road ahead was going to be tough; he had no illusions. Now, though, he knew he would win! He pulled his battered safari cap, his dusty and scratched companion that had witnessed it all, down tight on his head against the wind and softly hummed the nickel moon.

As the helicopter banked and crossed the Lake of Stars, Andy's final words echoed in his thoughts.

"THE GREATEST ADVENTURE IS THE REST OF YOUR LIFE!"

The End of the Beginning

"The temperature outside is 65 degrees with a high of around 74 expected today. Humidity is currently at 14 percent."

"Does that mean I can wear shorts this afternoon, Ted?"

"Well, you just can't run around town naked, you know, there are laws!"

"What if I stay in my car?"

"Denver is a friendly town, but not that friendly, you turkey!"

The radio talk show co-hosts bantered their light chat right up until Jim flipped the off button and slid the glass door aside to step out onto the redwood deck of his home. In the two weeks since he returned, he had healed rapidly.

His body was adjusting to the low humidity and cooler temperatures. Even though summer had begun, the cool air off the Rocky Mountains was a far cry from the sultry African jungle.

Jim stretched, arching his back with his arms raised high over his head and let out the stiffness with a loud groan of pleasure. He breathed the strong scent of the pine trees through his nose and exhaled through his mouth.

Strolling to the picnic table he sat down the book he was reading. *The Call of The Wild*, by Jack London, announced the cover. The book mark (the wrapper off the last candy bar he had found in his pack), showed he was halfway through the Alaskan adventure. He couldn't wait to get back to mushing his team.

This was the fourth book he had read since exiting the jungle, beginning with a copy of Josh McDowell's *More than A Carpenter*. He had found the fascinating book in the drawer of his room in the African hospital where he had spent the first three days before flying home. The doctors were reluctant to tell him about his condition at first.

He had suffered a concussion, probably from the fall down the cliff and colliding with the stone. Even more serious was the fact that infection had set in from the cuts. He was running a dangerously high fever when admitted. They supposed he would have fainted and died if he had remained lost for another twenty-four hours!

"Okay, make room, here we come!"

Jim turned to see his son, daughter, and wife stepping through the sliding glass door onto the deck. The small parade of big smiles was lead by his son, Roger, carrying a plate of pastries, his daughter, Claire, with a tray of mugs, and Tracey, so pretty in her rarely worn "special fancy apron," with a pot of his favorite coffee and a slender glass carafe of milk.

"Whoa, what's the occasion?" laughed Jim.

"It's your anniversary, Daddy," stated Claire as she sat a mug in front of every place.

Jim's eyes popped open wide and his mind raced. "Oh, no Tracey, I didn't forget...did I? Our anniversary is in March...isn't it?"

"Daddy, you fuzzball, not your wedding anniversary. It is your Been-Home-For-Two-Weeks anniversary!" His daughter patted his head, then decided to give him a little hug, a huge show of affection for the "soon to be a woman."

Tracey smiled as her eyes met Jim's.

"Of course," he laughed, "how could I have forgotten. What do we have here?"

"Mom made her awesome cherry turnovers and your stinky Star Butts coffee!" announced Roger.

"Starbucks," corrected Claire.

"Whatever," said the boy around a mouthful of turnover. "Dad, are we still going to the Rockies baseball game tomorrow?"

"A promise is a promise, son. I ordered the tickets with my credit card already. We've got some awesome seats. Look, I have the diagram here," Jim said, unfolding a color brochure of the field.

"Coooooool," said Roger, visualizing the field.

Tracey smiled again at her husband, her beautiful eyes peering over the coffee cup she held with both hands and slipped slightly. When they met at the airport as he came back from Africa, she had embraced him physically and emotionally. Never a word was spoken about the threat of divorce.

As Jim healed and they interacted with small conversations, Jim showed her a soft side she had never seen. After he was up and around, he had come to her as she brushed her hair one evening. He kneeled at her side by the little antique dressing table and pleaded for her love, apologizing for his role in the destruction of their intimacy and resisting the temptation to bring up her part in the problems.

It was awkward and embarrassing to speak like this after years of distance but the awful dread disappeared as the words tumbled out. Tears and confessions turned to a one long, long hug.

He gave her the letter he had written all alone atop the waterfall. She sighed and said she would give him a chance, after all, he sure was trying.

Since then they had been very easy together and why not? They had years of shared experiences to bond them and, of course, the children.

The four of them sat on the deck together and enjoyed the food, the view, the crystal clear mountain air, and their new old family.

"Oops!" shouted Roger plopping down his second pastry and wiping his mouth with a napkin then quickly licking his fingers before wiping them on his pants leg. "I almost forgot."

He reached into his pocket and pulled out a tattered envelope. "This came in the mail for you this morning, Dad." He handed his father the letter.

It was an international envelope with the red and blue hash marks on white paper. Apparently it had a rough journey, evidenced by lots of creases, folds, and a few scuff marks. Though the return address was Benjamin's name and American address, the stamps and postmark were African. It had been mailed almost two weeks ago.

"What is it honey?" asked Tracey as she watched Jim turn the small invitation sized letter over in his hands without opening it.

"I'm not sure," he said quietly.

"Well, Kreskin, are you going to mind read it or open it?" Roger cracked.

Jim looked down at his smart aleck son who was grinning broadly at his own joke, food stuck to his teeth. Jim had his work cut out for him in taming this kid.

"Oh, ha-ha," Claire chided her brother. "Go ahead Daddy, open it."

Jim rapped the envelope once on the table to push the letter inside down to the end then carefully tore the edge off. Shaking the contents out, a small single folded sheet landed on the table.

As he unfolded it, the letterhead for the Lake Of Stars Lodge crested the top. Jim quickly read the two handwritten paragraphs as his family watched, suspended in silence.

Without speaking or moving the letter from in front of him, Jim raised his head slowly and stared out toward the mountains, his thoughts thousands of miles away.

The children looked at their father, then at Tracey. Finally Tracey spoke for them all. "Honey, what is it?"

Jim tried to speak but choked and halted. His face was flushed. He turned to his family with a haunted painful look. He met their eyes one by one, then looked away back at the mountains. A tear formed then headed down his face as he spoke in a raspy voice.

"Weinberg," he began, "Weinberg is still alive."

Long after they had consoled him and returned to the house, he sat on the deck with Weinberg's old tattered Bible and thought about Africa.